Revelation

To Emily,

You are a friend who, almost without fail, can make me laugh. Your bizarre antics brightened many a day for me. I hope we stay friends and continue to bring light to each other's lives.

I love you,
awesome nerd.

Rhiannon Davies

Revelation

Rhiannon Davies

Edited by Denise de la Cruz

Dryad Publishing
2015

First Printing: 2015

ISBN 978-1-329-06594-9

Dryad Publishing
9024 Crestmoor Dr
Saint Louis, Missouri 63126

www.dryadpublishing.com

Dedication

To my friends, family, and teachers:
Thank you. I wouldn't have been able to to this without you.

Contents

Acknowledgements ix
Prologue 1
Chapter One 3
Chapter Two 10
Chapter Three 16
Chapter Four 24
Chapter Five 30
Chapter Six 42
Chapter Seven 47
Chapter Eight 56
Chapter Nine 62
Chapter Ten 69
Chapter Eleven 81
Chapter Twelve 93
Chapter Thirteen 100
Chapter Fourteen 111
Chapter Fifteen 122
Chapter Sixteen 133
Chapter Seventeen 148
Chapter Eighteen 154
Chapter Nineteen 155
Chapter Twenty 164
Coming Soon! 169
About the Author 170

Acknowledgements

It's a miracle this book was even finished; I would not have been able to do any of this on my own. My friends cheered me on during National Novel Writing Month to finish this, and sometimes physically restrained me so I couldn't run away from the computer. I'd like to thank Denise de la Cruz in particular, for editing this mess and making it halfway decent. She also provided the amazing cover. Megan Roegner provided me with the motivation to both finish writing and actually publish *Revelation*. Joy Mersmann, Abby Dorsey, and Kelly Winkleman got me into this mess in the first place. I'd also like to thank Karon Vandas and my parents for getting excited about my book, even when I really wanted to burn it. To Juliette Zach, I'd like to thank her for giving me at least one guaranteed reader. To Jennifer Sights, thank you for guiding me through the publishing process for the first time; you are invaluable.

Last, but not least, I'd like to thank Mark Pellegrino, whose fierce defence of Lucifer gave me a new perspective, and inspired me to write this novel.

Thank you all; it's been an amazing journey.

Prologue

Bodies lay strewn across the once-shining fields of Heaven, ashy feathers drifting slowly in the celestial currents. Two winged figures clashed in the distance, hovering on the edge of the battlegrounds. Resplendent in their star-forged armour, Michael and Lucifer wove around each other, striking at each other lightning-quick. Gabriel and Raphael struck down Azazel and Beelzebub before making their way toward the other two archangels.

Michael parried a lethal swipe of his brother's sword. "Why, brother? Why did you do this? Why could you not simply be content with humans the way they are?"

Lucifer snorted, whirling away from a thrust. "Because it doesn't make sense, Michael. Why would God leave His greatest creations wallowing in the mud? I did what He asked of me."

"He ordered that humans would remain innocent!"

"He *supposedly* ordered that humans would remain ignorant! Those that He made in His image!" Lucifer shook his head. "He also asked that we would love humans above all else—even Himself. I love them enough to go against Heaven. How much do you love them, Michael?"

"That's not the point—" Michael tried to reason.

"Of course that's the point!" Lucifer stepped back and tossed his blade aside. He spread his arms. "You want to kill me, fine. Just—" He took a deep breath. "Something is *wrong* in Heaven, Michael. When was the last time any of us even saw Father? I know when I did. He told us to look at the humans and love them. Who knows if the last few orders even came from Him? Please, if you listen to nothing else, listen to this." He waited.

Michael sighed and lowered his blade. "I'm not going to kill you, Lucifer. But you went against Heaven, and you know what the punishment for that is." He shook his head. "I'm sorry."

Lucifer lifted his chin and braced himself. Michael nodded and stepped forward. Gripping Lucifer's throat, Michael reached into the Veil-between-Worlds and opened the Gate to the Hell-Cage.

"Michael," Gabriel spoke up, sounding panicked. "Shouldn't we—"

Lucifer heard Raphael shushing him, but didn't look away from Michael. He could see the pain this was causing his older brothers; he just couldn't do anything about it.

Michael's eyes gleamed with unshed tears, but didn't blink. He couldn't look away from the youngest archangel, not now. He owed him that much. He inhaled deeply, preparing to throw Lucifer into the deepest pits of Hell—

And then all any of them knew was pain.

Chapter One

A horn blared from the driveway of the large Victorian. Rowan Fitzgerald tripped over her shoes in the hallway and cursed. As far as first days went, this one sucked already. Her alarm hadn't been reset for the school year, her bag wasn't packed, and she swore every single thing she owned had rearranged and hidden themselves.

Finally managing to do up the laces on her boots, Ro sprinted out the door, yelling a quick goodbye to the rest of the house. She threw herself into the backseat of the blue FRS Scion, panting.

"What took you so long?" her best, and only, girl friend asked dryly.

Ro glared half-heartedly at Carmen. "It's the first day of sixth year. Did you get a new car?" she asked, leaning forward into the front.

"Yes, I did," Gabriel replied curtly. "Now put your seatbelt on, I don't want to get arrested."

She leaned back, smirking. "Give a bloke a car, and suddenly he's no fun anymore."

"No, I'm pretty sure that's just Gabe. Anthony and Kali gave it to him to 'compensate' for not graduating early," Lucifer snickered, twisting to grin at Ro. She smiled back at the younger twin, resolutely ignoring the strange fluttering in her stomach.

"Mike and Rafe are worse," Carmen spoke up, shooting a knowing look at Ro.

Ro ignored it. "Mike and Rafe are huge mother hens that freaked out if we crossed the street without looking both ways half a dozen times."

"True," Luce sighed. "It's going to be weird, not having them around."

"Well, we're going to have to get used to it," Gabe said. "Kelso High, here we come."

The school wasn't ugly, really, even if it did have the unimaginative name emblazoned across the front. It had four large brick buildings: a gym, a music hall, a canteen, and classrooms, linked by glass covered walkways. There were a few fields out back for the sports teams, and the canteen opened into the courtyard nestled in the centre of the school.

"I'll see you at lunch, alright?" Carmen hugged Ro and slapped the brothers Elohim upside the head. "Try to wait at least a week before you start pranking, please?"

The innocent looks were far too transparent. They weren't even trying.

"Come on, Luce. We've got mostly the same schedule, except for electives. Gabe, we'll see you later." Ro waved before walking off, Luce catching up with her a few steps later.

"Where's your locker?" he asked, dodging a bus mob. She shrugged.

"Don't know, don't really care."

"Oh, yes, I forgot. 'Lockers are for wimps,'" he smirked.

Ro huffed and let the door fall on him. "I never said that. I just don't want to have my stuff in some metal container in the middle of nowhere."

"Kelso isn't exactly a big school, Ro," he said dryly. "Your locker will be right down the hall from most of your classes, not in the wastelands of Sweden."

"Where did Sweden come from?"

"I think the Trojans had something to do with it..." Luce dodged Ro's swipe at his head and continued. "It was the first thing I thought of. And it's nowhere near Kelso. Don't change the subject. You just want to do your homework in your other classes."

She shrugged, setting her messenger bag on the floor beside her desk. "Sue me. I would rather be doing other stuff after school than homework. Besides, I can multitask. Being smart enough to do that is kind of why they let me skip two years."

Luce opened his mouth to reply, but the door opening cut him off. The teacher, a small, mousy man wearing tweed and bifocals and looking like a walking stereotype of an Oxford professor (though what he would be doing in the Scottish Borders, Ro had no idea), bustled into the room and immediately launched into his lecture.

"I expect you all to remember last year's material, so we will jump right into vectors. Now, who can tell me…?"

Ro slumped onto the picnic bench, groaning as her head hit the table. Luce patted her on the back in mock sympathy as Carmen and Gabe joined them.

"What's wrong with her?" Gabe asked, frowning. They relaxed when Luce just grinned at them.

"Sixth year is making it impossible for Ro to multitask," he informed them with no small amount of glee in his voice. Ro swatted clumsily at him, lifting her head a few millimetres to glare balefully.

"It's supposed to be fourth year that's all the hard work. Why are they doing this to us? Don't we deserve a break?"

"Sure. It's called summer holidays," Carmen said, pulling out her lunch. Unlike most of the school, Carmen packed her own food instead of buying the 'canteen plastic.' "You could just pay attention like most people, instead of trying to do as much work as possible in as little time as possible."

"Boring," Ro huffed, letting her head thump back down. She mumbled something else.

"What?" Gabe looked confused, out of practice translating Ro-table-speak.

She huffed and sat up properly. "I said, 'How are your classes, then?'"

"Well, we aren't insane like you and Luce, so we only took a couple of Advanced Higher classes as opposed to every single one available," Carmen ribbed. "But I'm enjoying my computer class the most."

"Are you teaching it?" Luce asked.

"Better question: how many people, companies, governments, and militaries have you hacked yet?" Ro raised an eyebrow.

"I'm insulted. Do you really think I would do that?"

"Yes." The answer came in stereo.

"Seriously, people? If the Elohims have to wait a week to prank, then I have to wait a week to start hacking from school property. That's just how it works."

"If you say so. We have English next, right?" Luce rummaged around in his backpack for his schedule.

"Yep. Honestly, you have the nerve to call me disorganized? At least I have a system," Ro rebuked. The three stared, fascinated, as Luce pulled out book after book after folder after paper.

"How can you have this much crap already? It's the first day of the school year!" Gabe asked his brother, incredulous. "Seriously, you're as bad as Ro!"

"I don't hoard. And again: *organization*, Luce."

"I am organized! It just…multiplies."

"Yeah, okay little brother. We should—" Gabe broke off at a chirping noise and pulled his mobile out. He grinned and put it on the table before answering.

"You know, just because you're not in school anymore doesn't mean everyone else isn't either. Where are you?"

"Edinburgh. And don't pull that trick; unless the schedule has radically changed—which it hasn't in several years—it's lunch hour at the moment," Michael's tinny voice came through the speaker. Raphael laughed. "What are you crazy kids up to?"

Ro snorted. "You're calling us crazy? We haven't even done anything yet!"

"Yet? Not exactly reassuring, Rowan," Mike told her, amused. She rolled her eyes, sitting back on the bench.

"You just rolled your eyes at us, didn't you?" Raphael asked.

"I hate you both."

"No, you don't. We're bringing back souvenirs," Mike added.

"We all love you," Carmen said quickly, cutting Ro off. Ro pouted.

"When are you coming back?" Luce finally spoke, strangely quiet.

"A few more months, by Christmas at the latest. Rafe wants to go to London," Mike teased. "Everything okay?"

Luce blinked. "Of course. Why wouldn't it be?"

"Well, it's sixth year, for one. That was never very fun," Rafe mused.

"Yeah, Ro's already complaining," Gabe smirked. "The bell's about to ring, but it was good talking to you, bros."

"We'll have a party when you get back," Carmen added warmly. Ro made a noise of agreement, eyeing Luce with a contemplative expression.

"Talk to you lot later, then," Mike said, hanging up seconds later.

"*Are* you okay?" Ro asked suddenly, tilting her head as she frowned at Luce.

"What?" Luce frowned back at her. "Yes, of course. For now, at least. If we don't hurry, we're going to be late." He slung his bag over his shoulder, walking towards the classrooms. Ro frowned harder after him. Carmen nudged her with her shoulder, smiling softly when Ro looked at her and jerking her head in the direction of the school.

They followed the boys at a slower pace, Carmen trying to reassure her friend. "I'm sure it's nothing, Ro. You can interrogate him later if you like, but we really do have to get to—what?"

Ro had stopped, staring at the car-park. Carmen followed her gaze, catching sight of a suited albino man no one had ever seen before (and it was a relatively small town, everyone knew everyone in some context) standing beside Gabe's car. And he was staring back at them.

"Ro," Carmen said slowly. "Let's go inside, yeah? If he's still here when school's out, then we'll tell someone, okay? Just leave it for now. Please?"

For a moment, it seemed Ro was ignoring her. She reached out to her best friend, freezing when she startled. They stared at each other for a moment before looking back to the car-park—where the man was gone.

"That was weird," Ro muttered. She shook her head sharply. "Let's go to class."

Carmen sighed, glancing over her shoulder and furrowing her brow. She had an itch on the back of her neck, as if someone was still watching her. She jogged to catch up with Ro, firmly telling herself she'd worry about it later if she had to, or if it happened again. She shivered at that thought, sliding into a chair next to Gabriel.

"Where were you?" Gabe whispered as the teacher began to pass out papers.

"Just talking to Ro about something," she whispered back. Carmen didn't want her friends to be on edge about it as well. It was probably just a fluke.

"So, you are coming over today, right?" Ro asked as the final bell rang.

Carmen rolled her eyes. "Just like every other year, Ro. We're not going to break tradition our last year here."

"What are we going to do when we start university?" Gabe wondered.

Luce shrugged and rolled his eyes. "I suppose we'll figure it out when we get there. And besides, your family loves us more," Luce added. Gabe smirked.

"Especially since Mike and Rafe aren't around. When they get back—what happened to my car?" Gabe stopped abruptly, hands clenching in anger.

The four stared dumbly at the tires—the *slashed* tires.

"One of the other kids?" Carmen tried hopefully. Going by Ro's suspicious hum, it was convincing her about as much it convinced Carmen.

"Great," Gabe said flatly. "Kali's gonna kill me."

"Kali won't. Anthony might," Luce predicted gloomily.

"They're just tires. Get them replaced at the shop," Ro suggested.

"Yeah, and within five minutes the whole town will know. Not the best plan. Just call them; you're a victim, they'll understand," Carmen urged.

"You make it sound like I was mugged or something."

"Might as well have been. Or at least your car was. I guess we're walking home?" Luce asked, looking around.

Carmen shrugged. "Guess so."

"I called the shop, by the way. They'll be here in a few minutes," Ro said, patting Gabe sympathetically on the shoulder as he moaned pitifully. "Don't be such a baby."

Carmen rolled her eyes. "Come on, let's go. Ro, isn't your grandmother making those cookies with the jam on top?"

Ro nodded. "The Thumbprint ones, yeah. She's on a baking spree. Grandmother Lilly said we could be test-tasters if we get there before she gives them all away."

"What's she giving them away for?" Luce asked curiously, hefting his bursting bag onto his shoulder. "Didn't the town just have a charity event?'

Ro shook her head. "Yeah, but I think it's a church thing. Just because we're Wiccan doesn't mean we don't help the community. Still, I want some."

"Me, too," the others chorused, laughing. They crossed the street, heading down into the older part of town. Luce turned to Ro, barely hiding a smirk.

"So, what did you think of the English syllabus?" he asked, trying to keep a straight face.

"What's that supposed to mean?" She arched an eyebrow.

"He means the material. They put a lot of religious work on here this year," Carmen said.

"Dante's *Inferno* and Milton's *Paradise Lost*? Yeah, I know." Ro shook her head. "That's going to be an adventure."

"On the bright side, we don't start for a couple of weeks, and Milton's the first," Gabe remarked cheerfully.

"Yay," Ro deadpanned.

"Don't be a downer," Carmen chided. "Now get a move on, I want cookies."

Ro grinned suddenly. "Race you!"

"Cheater!" Luce shouted as Ro took off, Gabe hot on her heels. He glanced exasperatedly at Carmen before rolling his eyes as they followed, laughter carrying in the wind.

Chapter Two

"So, what *did* you think?" Luce asked a week later, as they were walking home. Gabe had gotten his tires replaced; as expected, Kali didn't care about the damage so much as finding the culprit and tearing reparations from their innards, and Anthony was indifferent once Gabe promised to pay for the job himself. He and Carmen had stayed after school to talk to the guidance counsellor about switching classes, so Ro and Luce decided to enjoy the relatively warm weather and walk home instead of waiting the few minutes for their friends.

"Of *Paradise Lost*? It's interesting, to say the least," Ro replied absently. "I like Lucifer."

"Of course you do. Won't the rest of your family be upset?" Luce teased.

"Shut up," she said, shoving him. "None of us are religious, per se. Christianity has a lot of problems, but as far as the angels are concerned, Lucifer is my favourite. Gabriel's a close second, though."

"Why?" Luce cocked his head, bewildered. "I mean, he's the devil, Satan. Lucifer went against God and fell; he's the embodiment of pure *evil*."

Ro glared at him. "He is not evil! He just—" She stopped walking and turned to face him, brushing an auburn curl out of her eyes. "Look. Lucifer is the Morningstar, the Light-bringer. He was the brightest angel of Heaven. Angels were literally made of love, to love, by the greatest source of love in the universe. Logically, it follows that Lucifer possessed the second greatest capacity for love. It makes sense that he loved humans enough to fall for them. It makes absolutely no sense that God punished him for doing exactly what he asked."

"He didn't, though," Luce pointed out. "He went against a direct order and told Eve to eat from the Tree of Knowledge. God didn't want them to have that kind of power."

Ro rolled her eyes. "So God, who made humans in his image, wanted them to remain ignorant beasts for the rest of their short existence? And speaking of image, God obviously isn't perfect. Humans make mistakes all the time."

Luce stared. "Did you even read the Bible?"

She huffed and started walking again. "The Bible written by humans? I read the first couple pages before I got completely lost. Why would God put humans 'in dominion' over all other creatures and life on earth? They don't even do a very good job of taking care of themselves."

Luce decided to ignore that last part. "Yeah, well, it's pretty clear that Lucifer was punished for his disobedience as God intended. And besides, logic and faith don't always operate by the same rules." Luce jogged to catch up with her, turning onto their street.

"I get the grounding, I do—"

"*Grounding?*"

"—don't get me wrong, but forcing him to leave home, with no chance for forgiveness? I was under the impression that God was all about the forgiving."

Luce gaped, stopping on his lawn. "Do you take some perverse pleasure in mutilating Christianity?"

"Hey, don't take it personally, I'll judge anything that doesn't make sense. I'm not even technically Wiccan, remember? More spiritual and Druid-like: respecting the power, but not necessarily worshipping gods who may or may not have given it to us." Ro leaned against the giant old oak in the middle of her yard and grinned at him.

"Yeah, okay. I have homework." He turned to go inside, and then paused. "Do you want to come in now or later?"

Ro shook her head. "I'm going to stay outside for a while. It's nice; the town's energy has a clear flow for once."

"Sometimes, I swear you're making this up off the top of your head," Luce teased.

Ro bristled. "Sometimes, I swear you don't actually respect me at all," she snapped, pushing off the tree and striding towards her house.

Luce winced. "Oh, come on, Ro, you know I didn't mean it like that!" he called after her.

"Do I?" She didn't stop, and slammed the door behind her.

"Oh, man, bro, you messed up big," his annoying brother snickered behind him. Throwing an arm around his shoulders, Gabe promptly let Luce take all his weight. "She's gonna be mad for *weeks*."

"Thank you, Gabe, for your rousing support," Luce deadpanned.

"I am very supportive. I'm Team Ro. That was a moronic move on your part."

"You think I don't know that? Get off," he grumbled, dragging himself and Gabriel up the steps and opening the door. He promptly dropped both bag and brother to the carpet.

"You know you love me. No one can resist this face," Gabe grinned. Luce shook his head in resigned amusement, stubborn as always. "Seriously, though, Luce. You should just ask her out already."

Luce sputtered. "*What!*"

"Bro, everyone can see it. You can't see straight around her and ignore all other girls, and she ignores pretty much anyone else. Or she bites their head off when they 'intrude.'" Gabe rolled his eyes as Luce stood frozen in the hallway. "You've known each other since forever ago, how hard can it be to ask her out on a date?"

Luce flailed. "Exactly! Ro's my best friend, I can't lose that!"

"You won't have to, idiot. If you don't ask, she will, I guarantee it." Gabe cuffed him upside the head as he moved into their kitchen. Rummaging around for the tooth-rotting snack he was craving, Gabe snuck a worried glance at his twin brother.

Luce had developed into the average hormonal boy about a month or so ago, and proceeded to angst like the professional emo he was. Genuine smiles that lasted more than three seconds Gabriel's little brother reserved for Ro alone. Michael leaving on his road trip hadn't helped, either. Of all the Elohim brothers, the eldest and youngest had a bond forged from protecting each other in the orphanage. Raphael and Gabriel had handled their own problems, but Michael and Lucifer had often stepped in to help the other fight their battles. That reliance hadn't changed years later.

Straightening up, he turned back to Luce who had chosen a stool at the island. Through a mouthful of chocolate caramel popcorn, Gabe imparted his last gem of wisdom, ignoring the disgusted expression the other boy wore. "Besides, if you don't get your act together, someone else is going to ask her out. Or you. Trust me; you don't want that to happen. Girls are vicious when they want revenge. 'Hell hath no fury,' and all that." He thumped Luce on the shoulder on his way out the door. "Good luck. Catch you later, bro."

Luce groaned and let his head thunk onto the countertop. "I'm gonna die."

"Hardly. He's right, though," Carmen said, reappearing from her detour to Ro's house. "She likes you, you like her: you're both just being stupid at this point."

"As much as I appreciate your unsolicited advice, I'm not prepared to risk our lifelong friendship to become secondary school sweethearts," Luce snapped.

Carmen frowned at him. "Maybe you had better ask Ro what she wants, instead of just assuming—"

"Carmel, did you get caught by the NCA?" Gabe called from the front room. The two joined him from the kitchen.

"Ignoring the blatant insult there, why are you asking?" Gabe just pulled aside the sheer drapes on the window, revealing a man in a suit. Carmen inhaled sharply.

"You recognize him? Are we going to jail?" Luce panicked.

Carmen shook her head. "Ro and I saw him before, standing by your car." She frowned. "Actually, I think it was right after lunch, just before the tires got slashed."

"That's the tosser that slashed my tires? He owes me six hundred bucks!" Gabe yelled, striding furiously to the door.

"Wait, you don't know who he is! He could be a federal agent or a private investigator or a paedophilic serial killer or something!" Carmen whispered frantically, grabbing Gabe's arm.

"Doesn't matter. He's gone," Luce reported. Gabe rushed back to the window, peering out at the empty street.

"He did that before, too. He just stood there and watched us, we looked away, and the next moment he was gone," Carmen said.

"I didn't look away or blink or anything. He literally just vanished into thin air," Luce said, furrowing his brow.

"Okay. Maybe we should talk to Ro about this," Carmen offered nervously. "Earlier, she definitely seemed to recognize him. Or at least recognize whatever he is."

"Yeah, that's a good plan. You talk to her; I'm pretty sure she's not feeling too accommodating towards the Elohim family." Gabe pointedly shoved his elbow into his brother's ribs.

"What did you do?" she asked, scowling at the youngest brother.

Luce winced. "I made a mistake, was an insensitive prat, and hit a sore spot."

Carmen raised an eyebrow. "You insulted her Wiccan abilities again, didn't you?"

"It may have been implied that they don't exist?"

She bristled, clearly furious. "Damn it, Luce, you *know* how sensitive she is about that! Just because she hasn't shown any signs of active magic and it's almost her sixteenth birthday—"

"Doesn't mean she's inert. I *know* she's going to powerful! I know it usually takes a strong emotional or stressful experience to bring out latent magic, and just because nothing has happened yet doesn't mean it won't, or that she won't come into her own on her birthday. I shouldn't have said anything, and I'm going to apologize. After she's cooled that distinctive Scottish temper of hers, of course," Luce added, flinching.

Carmen glared as Gabe snickered in the background. "You are a coward, Lucifer Elohim. Maybe if you actually had a meaningful conversation with her, you two wouldn't have so many problems. I'm going to talk to my best friend, and we're going to have a girl's night. If either of you intrude, I'll help Ro skin your nether regions and force them down your throat." She spun on her heel and marched out the door, ignoring the dumbstruck looks in her wake.

"Girls," Luce said slowly, "are absolutely, completely insane."

His brother gripped the back of his neck. "Welcome to your future, little brother," Gabe said solemnly, before grinning and shoving his head away. Luce growled and playfully tackled his brother over the couch. They broke apart, laughing, when they hit the floor.

"Come on." Gabe pulled Luce to his feet. "If they're having a girl's night, we're going to order pizza and play video games all night."

"Don't you have homework? I have homework," Luce tried, twisting in Gabe's grip.

"For once, Luce, just be a normal boy: shirk your responsibilities, clog your arteries with cholesterol, and rot your brain with mindless digital violence." Gabe shoved Luce down in front of the television and slapped a controller in his hands. "Trust me; it'll be fun!"

Chapter Three

"He's moping," Gabe declared, plopping down beside Carmen in second period Algebra II. She frowned.

"Ro took the Mackie's Chocolate Ice Cream Therapy route," Carmen sighed. "This is out of control. They're just hurting each other, and I've never seen it get this bad."

"I know," Gabe said. "I mean, they've fought and insulted each other before, sure, but they make up in a few days. There's something deeper going on here."

"We should just lock them in a closet," Carmen mused. "They need to resolve their sexual tension and stop tormenting the rest of us."

Gabe glanced at her, surprised. "That's what you think this is about? UST? You haven't noticed anything else…off?"

She eyed him suspiciously. "Not really. Why, have you?"

He grimaced, hastily marking down his homework when the teacher walked by them. "Luce has been really quiet lately. I mean, he's always been the quietest brother, but this is more like…he's scared or worried about something, and he's not telling anyone and it's eating him up inside. I don't know what's going on with him."

"Maybe he's just missing Mike. Hasn't he always gone to Michael whenever he had major problems?" Carmen pointed out gently.

Gabe sighed. "Could be. I just don't like not knowing what's going on with him, and that he feels he can't tell me."

She patted his arm reassuringly. "Whatever it is, I'm sure it can't be too bad. If something truly awful happened, he'd let one of us know. Otherwise we'd kick his arse from one end of the universe to the other."

"Yeah, I guess." Gabe grimaced at the teacher glared at them. "We'll just have to wait and see, apparently."

Carmen smiled at Gabe. Most of the time, people overlooked him for his brothers. Not many people bothered to get to know Gabriel, or thought he wasn't worth it, especially compared to the rest of his family. Carmen had always tried to do the exact opposite, never abandoning Gabriel and being there for him when he was overwhelmed or depressed. Yet for all that, Gabe still tried so hard to build relationships and "get in" with the popular kids who would either use him and throw him away, or degrade and dismiss him.

More often than not, Carmen felt like Gabe ignored her like others did to him. If he would just pay attention, if he got to know her a little better, the girl under the façade she showed everyone else, then maybe…

Maybe they would crash and burn and she'd get her heart broken. Who was she kidding? Gabriel Elohim would never think of her as anything more than Ro's best friend.

Dry lightning illuminated the edges of town, a faint rumble of thunder echoing in Gabriel's chest shortly after. Though still far off, the storm would be here by tonight. His Maltese jumped up and burrowed beneath his comforter, nearly dislodging his MacBook Air.

"Noah, careful! It's bad enough the car got damaged, I don't need to deal with more broken, *expensive* things," Gabe scolded. Noah peeked out and whined.

Gabe melted. "Oh, come on, you know I didn't mean it like that. I love you more than any cold, dead piece of technology. I just can't afford to have Kali and Anthony mad at me. That means finishing my homework this time before playing. And I need a working computer for that."

"He misses you," his adoptive mom spoke up from the doorway. "He's a living creature that needs attention. You can make time for him if you need to."

Kali was one of those women that people would never expect to be the motherly type, or to find in a small town. Tall, with smooth cocoa skin, straight and shiny black hair that hung to her waist either loose or in a braid, classic aristocratic features, and cool amber eyes combined to make an actress out of a Bollywood film. She only ever accented her beauty with elegant suits and dresses, a little lipstick, and a well-maintained body.

Gabriel often wondered, especially when he and his brothers had first come here, why someone like Kali would ever adopt four brothers. Or live here. Actually, there was a lot Gabe wondered about Kali, though it had never seemed all that important to ask her. Like how her beauty never seemed to decline, but she put no visible effort into maintaining her body. Or how she never worked, but managed to adopt and pay for four boys. And how she knew random bits of history his professors didn't mention, but she had no record of attending any university or ancient texts lying around the house.

"I'll take him out to the park when I'm finished writing my essay," he assured her. "Shouldn't take me too long."

Kali's lips quirked ever so slightly at one corner. For her, that was like a blinding grin. "Of course. Will this one be novel length as well?"

Gabe blushed and ducked his head. "No. I'm reserving my writing hand for—" He broke off, suddenly self-conscious. He hadn't told anybody about his side project yet; not even Carmen, who he shared almost everything with.

Kali raised one perfect eyebrow and crossed the room. She settled herself gracefully on the end of his bed, arranging her long limbs to her satisfaction before staring expectantly at him. "For…?"

Gabriel squirmed for a moment, uncomfortable under Kali's heavy gaze. He caved in under a minute. "It's just an idea I've been toying around with." Reaching into the bedside table, Gabriel pulled out a leather journal Michael had gotten for him last Christmas (also known as his birthday). He slid it across the bedspread, refusing to meet her eyes.

For the next several minutes, the only sounds in the room were pages flipping gently, keys clacking, and Noah's soft pants. Gabe hammered out a half-arsed conclusion, trying and failing not to worry about Kali's reaction, and nervously twisted his fingers into Noah's thick fur, restlessly petting the dog. When the book was set down on his keyboard, Gabe still didn't look up.

A manicured finger tipped his chin up, and he hesitantly glanced at her. Kali was smiling. Not a quirk of the lips or a slight warming of her eyes, or a smirk, or the polite one she used on their neighbours; a real and true smile, small though it may be.

"Where did you get the ideas from?" she asked quietly.

Gabe shrugged. "I've...been having some weird dreams lately. They're disjointed, like they're happening out of order. I started writing them down a few weeks ago, which seems to make them flow better, at the very least."

Kali nodded. "You should keep writing them down. Perhaps start rewriting them in a more comprehensive manner?"

He looked at her, surprised. "What, like an actual story? I can't write about all of us like that. It's too weird." He shook his head. "And what would be the point? It's not like anyone else will ever read it."

She tilted her head to one side. "Won't they? Besides, don't most authors get their best ideas from dreams? You could just change the names." Kali eyed him carefully. "It is a brilliant idea, and letting talent like yours go to waste is a crime." She patted his knee once and stood. "At least try, Gabriel. If you decide it is not working, then fine. But do not give up before you've even started. Nothing great is ever accomplished that way."

Gabe sat there alone, stunned. His parents hardly ever gave out compliments, and certainly not for anything other than academic achievements. He gingerly picked up the journal, stroking the cover absently. Not many people knew about his passion for writing; he had worked hard to perfect the carefree, hedonistic rascal image. Still, perhaps Kali had a point. His musings were broken by Noah, who leapt onto his lap and promptly treated his face as a lollipop. Gabe pushed him off, laughing. He grabbed the leash and Noah's tennis ball, the dog immediately bounding down the stairs once he realized they were going out.

Gabriel let the leash stretch out to its fullest, his crazy dog trying to run everywhere at once. When they reached the end of the street, Noah started barking nonstop and straining across the road. Gabe huffed and let Noah drag him over, only realizing who the dog sensed when they were halfway there. Carmen crouched down to say hello, grinning at the Maltese. She completely ignored Gabriel.

He swallowed nervously, dry throat clicking. Wiping his hands on his jeans to prevent the leash slipping out of his sweaty grip, he tried for a casual smile.

"Hey Carmel," he croaked, wincing at the crack in his voice. She squinted up at him briefly, giving only a short "Hey" in response.

"Noah and I are going to the park," he tried again. Why was talking to Carmen outside of school alone always so hard? "Do you want to come throw a ball for us?"

Her eyebrows shot up as she rose. Noah whined and nosed her hand. "Are you going to be racing Noah for it?"

Gabriel's brow furrowed as he rewound the last few seconds of conversation. His eyes widened in realization. "With us! I meant *with* us! Or with me, really, because Noah can't throw the ball, and why would he—" *Shut up! Shut up, you idiot!* He stood there miserably as Carmen visibly tried not to laugh. *Great, she probably thinks you're ridiculous and stupid. She probably only hangs out with you because of Ro and Luce. It must be why you can't talk to her about anything* normal.

"Sure, I'd love to come throw a ball with you," Carmen said, voice barely level.

"Great," Gabe replied, mood dimming when he got a pity response. He hated people feeling sorry for him.

"So, have you talked to Luce any more?" she asked after a few minutes of walking in silence. He looked over at her, confused.

"About whatever's bothering him," she added hastily upon seeing his face. It cleared in understanding.

"Not really. What about Ro? Has she said anything about their falling out?" Gabe bent down to let Noah off his leash, the dog instantly sprinting away across the large field. He and Carmen stood at the end near the playground. Large woods threaded with hiking and biking trails comprised the rest of the park. Gabriel breathed deep, letting the cool air wash through him. Somehow, the park never failed to calm him down, like he became part of a world unaffected by petty human problems.

Carmen sighed. "No, and she's been avoiding him as well. Which should be impossible, since they have practically every class together."

Gabe rolled his eyes in agreement. "They've always been idiots, but this is particularly moronic, even for them." He pulled the ball out of his pocket, offering it to Carmen. She lightly tossed it up once before hurling it three-quarters of the field. Noah chased after it, trotting back for another go. Gabe threw it this time, and Noah took off again.

"Agreed. We need to get them to talk to each other. Civilly." Carmen chucked the ball again, and Noah darted away, clearly having the time of his life.

"So, what? *Should* we lock them in a closet?" Gabe asked, dubious. Carmen shook her head, handing the ball back to him.

"No, we just need to force them into a conversation; even if we have to play intermediary, at least they will be semi-communicating."

"I think you're overestimating their maturity," Gabe said dryly, throwing the ball as hard as he could. It landed at the tree line opposite them as Noah flopped down on his feet, panting heavily and slobbering everywhere. Gabriel frowned down at him severely as Carmen doubled over laughing. "You're going to make me go get that, aren't you?" The Maltese gave a happy little woof and rolled onto his back so Carmen could rub his belly—which she did, grinning mischievously up at him.

Gabe sighed, trudging to the end of the field to pick up the spit-and-dirt covered ball. He wiped it on the grass before sticking it back in his pocket. The wind began to pick up, whispering from the depths of the forest. The dark trees loomed, creaking and swaying towards him. For a moment, he almost swore something—*several* somethings—were rushing towards him on the branches. Gabe shivered and backed away quickly. Carmen had clipped Noah's leash to his collar, and refused to hand it over. They strolled back to her house, bracing themselves against the biting wind. A Scottish sunset in November tended to lower the temperature about ten degrees, even without a breeze.

"I'll see you tomorrow, Carmel," Gabe called, turning back up the street.

"Gabe!" He paused, turning back towards her. She smiled brightly. "I had fun today. Thanks." She waved, heading back into her house. He barely had the presence of mind to wave back, his voice and breath lost somewhere between his lungs and throat. No matter how hard he tried, he couldn't get the stupid grin off his face, even when it began to pour.

Luce jerked awake, terrified and feeling like he was falling, even though he was firmly in the middle of his bed. This latest nightmare…they had all been devastating, but this one had him fearing for his life. Or at least his dream life. Already, the memory of it was slipping away, but the feelings it left behind seeped deeper into his mind.

Mostly, the dreams were just blurs, flashes of colour and snatches of sound. Brilliant white-gold light, wings flapping and metal clanging; those bursts were all he could ever remember about these…episodes. While he'd occasionally been sick or depressed for a few minutes afterwards, the leftover feelings usually faded.

This one was different. The breathing exercises and systematic unclenching of his muscles did not work, and the blinding terror kept rising. Whatever threat he faced in his dreams, it almost felt like it was here, in his house or the immediate vicinity.

His panic was broken by four things happening at once: a scream, the ground shaking, a loud cannon blast, and an electric dome erupting from the house next door—Ro's house.

Luce leapt out of bed, tripping into Gabe as they both careened out of their rooms. Kali and Anthony strode through the door at the end of the hall, composed as ever.

The street had flooded with people by the time they finally made it outside. Ro and her Aunt Willow were pale and crying, the look alien on such normally strong women. Luce and Gabe wasted no time going to their friend, reaching her at the same time as Carmen, who had arrived from the next street over. The town's small emergency services force pulled into the street, the flashing lights reflecting off of the still-glowing dome around Ro's house.

"What *happened*?" Luce gaped, unable to tear his gaze away from the boundary. It parted to let the paramedics in, but refused the other citizens.

Ro shuddered, Willow wrapping an arm around her as she answered. "There was a man…the same man that was following us before, I think…he just *appeared* in front of Grandmother. She…the wards activated instantly, even though he shouldn't have been able to get anywhere near here in the first place…but he did something to her, he just *touched* her and she *collapsed* and she's not *moving…*" she trailed off, choking on a fresh wave of tears.

Luce's stomach felt like molten lead; he was pretty sure his face reflected the horrified looks the others wore. He made an aborted reach for Ro, not sure if it would be welcome. Before he could decide, Carmen gasped and stared, wide-eyed, at a point behind him. They turned.

Toby Gibbons, the town coroner, wheeled the stretcher cart down the porch steps, the edge of a white plastic sheet trailing on the ground. Ro made a little punched-out noise as her legs collapsed. Luce barely got his arms around her in time, sinking down to the grass as sobs wracked her body.

"Oh, *Ro*," Carmen whispered, thudding to her knees beside them and folding her grieving friend in a hug. Willow, Kali, and Anthony stood over the four of them, easily and quietly deflecting the officials and nosy neighbours. They stayed that way for more than an hour, holding vigil and supporting Ro as she finally went quiet and stared blankly into space.

Chapter Four

Ro stayed out of school for a week, the other three forced to return after a few days. Kali and Anthony were more lenient than the Feyes, but still refused to let them slack off their schoolwork for too long. They constantly worried over Ro when she wasn't with them, and the moment the weekend started they got Willow and their parents' approval to stay over at the Fitzgerald house.

Ro, for her part, had locked herself away in her room, researching and scribbling away in her Grimoire. Her grandmother's own 'magic manual' lay open in front of her, and dozens of other creature books spiralled out from the centre of her floor. No two were open to the same monster, but they all had two things in common: power, and some form of teleportation. Unfortunately, there were far more than she anticipated, and she was slowly going through and eliminating the choices. Demons, of course, were the most likely culprits, but her house was warded against those with evil intent, and demons were practically made of evil. Several other creatures were capable of teleportation and could kill with a touch, but again, the wards. Unless someone had disabled them somehow…

A knock on the door disrupted her concentration. Aunt Willow had brought her food periodically, but never knocked. She knew Ro wouldn't answer, and just barged in to make sure she wasn't dead and more or less taking care of herself. Which meant it was an official, a neighbour, or one of her friends.

"Come in," she called, clearing her throat roughly. The door cracked open and Luce peered around warily.

"Did you booby trap your room?" he joked, trying not to trip or dislodge any of the texts.

She frowned at him and shifted a pile. "I'm trying to figure out what was in my house. I knew he was different when we first saw him—"

"Right before he slashed my tires," Gabe grumbled, Carmen following him in. "You couldn't have stopped him, or warned me or something?"

"I didn't know what he was here for, and you'd be surprised how many different nonhumans come through town," Ro told him absently. "Usually it's just out of curiosity, or they don't know we're here. They leave pretty soon after. This one didn't."

"So, does that make him stupid or exponentially more powerful than your average monster?" Carmen mused.

"Either? Both? Neither?" Ro guessed. "I'm not sure yet. Hence the research."

"Ro," Luce said quietly. "How are you holding up?"

Ro went still and let her hair fall forward to block her face from them. "I'm doing as well as could be expected. Better with something to focus on, even if it is revenge. It might not be healthy, but it's better than sinking into depression and becoming a shadow of who I am. Grandmother wouldn't want that for me." She looked back up, defiance burning in her gold eyes. At that moment, she looked like a being made of fire, ready to scorch her enemies.

"Well, then, where do we start?" Gabe asked, plopping down on the floor next to her.

Ro blinked. "What?"

Carmen shook her head gently. "We loved Lilly too, Ro. Anything we can do to help, just ask."

"We're not going to let you do this alone, Ro," Luce declared. "You have others who love you and are willing to support you. Let us."

She glanced at each of them, seeing only earnest hope and serious dedication. Ro sighed. "Fine. Gabe, look up the different types of wards in my grandmother's Grimoire. Carmen, crosscheck those with the different types of creatures that could get past them. Luce, can you get on your laptop and research different creature abilities that way? I'm going to keep writing in my book."

Luce leaned forward and grasped her shoulder. "We'll figure this out, Ro. We're going to catch him, and we'll deliver justice when we do. Okay?"

Ro smiled at him weakly, but it was more than she had done all week. The other three exchanged looks, and then split away to their various tasks.

After the Elohims and Carmen had come over, Willow forced Ro to go back to school. She went, reluctantly, but spent all her spare time researching. At one point, she even brought her Grimoire to school. Luce had been covering for her as much as he could, but his friend seemed disinclined to help. Ro had dropped all other responsibilities, prioritizing her vengeance to the point of obsession. There were times when Luce thought the only reason she ate and slept at all was because they made her. Just the other day, he'd had to pull her out of the street when Ro had almost walked out in front of an oncoming car.

The three of them had tried to make sure someone was with Ro at all times, which was why Luce was walking home with her again. Carmen's parents had picked her up early for a dentist appointment, and Gabriel had stayed behind to retake a maths test. Due to his increased paranoia over his car, the other two were walking home. Again.

"How far have we gotten? With the narrowing down of the monsters, and everything," Luce asked haltingly. He hated to encourage the laser focus Ro had on her grandmother's killer, but she wasn't really willing to talk about anything else these days.

"Too far." When Luce eyed her carefully, wondering exactly how that was supposed to make sense, she hastily elaborated. "We have fewer and fewer choices, but it's not looking likely that anything we've found or thought about could have done what that *thing* did. I don't think anything less than a god could have gotten through our wards."

"Could it have been a god? I mean, you haven't warded against pagans—" He stumbled to a stop as Ro turned on him furiously.

"Pagans don't do this. The only way any of them can take the life of a Wiccan is if the sacrifice is willing. I know what I saw, Luce. Grandmother wasn't working a spell, she didn't give herself over as a sacrifice, and she was *scared.* He wasn't friendly, and he wasn't pagan. I know what that kind of energy feels like, and this was something completely different." Ro breathed in deeply, shaking. Luce wrapped an arm around her, changing course from their street to the church near the centre of town.

"Why are you taking me into a Christian church?" Ro mumbled into his chest. He shushed her gently and opened the door, letting warmth wash over them both. The pews were empty, the candles lit but the pastor nowhere to be seen. Weak winter light filtered in through the stained glass windows, throwing colourful patterns onto the wood floors.

Luce guided Ro to sit on one of the benches, kneeling beside her as she folded in on herself, gasping for breath. He glanced towards the sanctuary, the heavenly scene depicted above and behind drawing his eye. Jesus Christ shone from the centre, of course, with the four archangels hovering around him. Michael, Raphael, Gabriel, Uriel—

A sharp, blinding pain crushed Luce into the side of the pew. He bit down on a scream as it built, filling his mind until the pressure in his skull seemed like it would split him in half. He was dimly aware of the blood pouring from his ears and nose, but it was second place to the crescendo of bone-rattling music that almost sounded like a voice.

"Lucifer!" Ro's scream somehow made it through the noise. He squinted in her general direction, noting distantly that her blurry form wasn't where he left it on the bench. He grimaced and tried to crawl across the room to her, only for an invisible force to fling him into a statue of St. Christopher. He groaned and pushed a stone hand off of his leg, barely registering the dark form that loomed over him. It raised a limb and began to chant, the ground shaking beneath them from the strength of its power. Well, that, or from the blood loss.

Shadows rushed in from the edges of his vision, until he could only just make out vague shapes. For a few seconds before he fell into unconsciousness, he swore the figure had six large wings spreading from the centre of its back.

Ro had been jolted out of her breakdown when Luce screamed and began seizing. Unable to stop it, she had tried to keep him still, so he wouldn't hurt himself more. When blood began gushing from his head, she'd cursed the pastor of the church who clearly wasn't all that concerned with the possibly dying boy in his nave.

So preoccupied was she with Luce, Ro didn't realize another presence had entered the holy grounds until it was too late. The man—the same bastard who had killed her grandmother—glanced once in her direction before waving his hand and sending her crashing into the altar. She whimpered in pain as the man turned towards Luce—who was still insensible. Ro sucked in a deep breath and hacked a cough before hoarsely yelling Luce's name. No response.

"*Lucifer!*" He jerked at her scream and tried to move, only for the thing to throw him away like he had Ro. The creature strolled over to her best friend, chanting and holding out something towards Luce. A desperate anger began boiling Ro's gut, fuelled by the fear of losing yet another loved one—and Luce was the most important person in her life right now. The ground began shaking, and the fires around the room had outgrown their candles, but all Ro cared about was Luce and he *wasn't moving*—

Years of pent up power, slowly gathering and feeding off of the ambient magic layering the earth, burst out of Ro in a torrent of colour and strength. It screamed around the church, tearing at the walls and shattering the windows. The man turned away from her prone friend, raising a hand in defence and casting the shadows of freaking *wings* on the walls behind him. Her power whipped towards the man—*angel*—with such ferocity that it hurled him back through the presbytery.

Ro darted over and pulled Luce up. He was unconscious, though thankfully the bleeding had stopped. Red crusted his skin, hair, and clothes, and some of it flaked off onto Ro when she slung his arm over her shoulder. Her magic, still pulsing wild through the physical plane, supported Luce's other side. Ro steadied herself, gripped Luce tightly, and Walked.

Space bent around them, and the church disappeared. Luce fell forward past the wards, Ro stumbling after him. Aunt Willow burst out of the house, speaking frantically into her mobile as she slid to a stop beside them. Ro's heart, still beating hard from the adrenalin and the realisation of exactly what had killed her grandmother, jumped up and lodged itself in her throat as she took in just how pale he was. The clouds crossing the sun that moment only served to make him look more like a corpse.

Chapter Five

Kelso Community Hospital wasn't much: three floors, a few A&E rooms, one permanent ward, a labour unit, and the surgical/diagnosing rooms next to the morgue in the basement. Gabe was trying not to think about that area.

Ro seemed composed, to those who didn't know her. To her friends and family, she was barely holding herself together. The white knuckles and tight jaw was the only outward evidence of her emotional state.

"Lucifer Elohim?"

Gabe and Ro leapt to their feet before the second syllable was out, the parents, Willow and Carmen scrambling to keep up. They charged the nurse.

"How is he?"

"Can we see him?"

"What happened?"

"Do you know what did this?"

"Was this *intentional*?"

"Stop! Rowan, Gabriel, give the poor girl some breathing room. Now," Kali focused her attention on the nurse. "What can you tell us?"

The girl smiled shakily at her, hugging her clipboard to her chest. "Mr. Elohim will be fine. He is resting now, so you probably won't be able to see him until tomorrow morning. The doctors would like to keep him for a couple more days, for observation purposes, but then he can go home." She hesitated, and then blurted the rest as quickly as possible. "He had some damage to his inner ears, but the toxicology and brain scans look clean, so no lasting harm. His symptoms are similar to cases with exposure to noise levels beyond safe decibels, but besides that the police will deal with the situation."

"Why are the police getting involved?" Kali asked sharply. The nurse winced.

"There was…other trauma on your son's body. Signs of beating: multiple lacerations, deep bruising; luckily nothing fractured and no internal bleeding. If this was a fight at school—"

"It wasn't," Ro growled immediately. "Some stranger came into town a few months ago, attacked Luce and I in the church earlier today. He—"

The nurse held up a hand. "Please, unless you have information relevant to Mr. Elohim's medical condition, tell the police. That's their area of expertise."

She headed for the station, passing off the clipboard. Ro turned away in frustration, roughly running her hands through her hair. Anthony sighed heavily.

"I can take Carmen home, if you two will stay here with the children," he murmured in a low voice to Kali and Willow, face full of sympathy. The women evaluated the three teenagers, and nodded. Anthony stepped forwards and placed a callused hand on Carmen's shoulder.

"Your parents will be wanting you home soon," he reminded her gently. When she opened her mouth to protest, he squeezed gently. "You can do nothing more here tonight. Luce would not want you to suffer because of him. You need sleep; it's a school day tomorrow."

Ro groaned. "Stars above, I can't even *think* about school right now. Maybe we should just stay home." She looked hopefully at her aunt.

"Unless you somehow manage to ace all your finals by the next week, you have to go to school," Willow told her tartly. "I can't homeschool you, and socialization is a good thing."

Ro pouted. Gabe ignored them all, still staring at the doors to the rest of the hospital. Kali came to stand beside him, looking in the same direction.

"He's strong, Gabriel," she said quietly. "He's a fighter; he'll make it through this."

"I know he will," he muttered. "I just don't like that he has to go through it in the first place. Why would someone attack him?"

Kali shook her head, pensive. "I don't know. But we will figure this out, Gabriel. I promise you that."

Gabe glanced up at her. Assessing the fierce glint in her eyes, he smiled gratefully. For a moment, it had almost looked as if there were flames burning in the irises.

Luce blinked awake slowly, wincing at the bright fluorescents overhead. Eyes watering, it took him a few minutes to piece together what happened. The last thing he remembered was colliding with the statue, so it was probably safe to say he was in the hospital. He fumbled for the remote thingy that controlled hospital beds. Those existed, right? Not just in films and medical dramas…

They must have given him drugs. Luce would never have thought in loops like that otherwise. He managed to find it and hit a button at random. The bed jerked down. Luce hastily hit another button, this one thankfully raising the bed. He looked up carefully—

Only to find Ro's face centimetres from his own.

He yelped—or would have, if Ro hadn't clamped a hand over his mouth at the last second. He glared at her, and she looked steadily back at him before releasing him.

"What are you *doing* here?" he hissed. She ignored him, getting up and going back to…painting the walls? "Scratch that, what are you doing, period?"

"Warding the room. It's ancient Enochian, so more powerful than anything else Wiccans have ever used; I just hope it can keep the angel out." Ro finished drawing a sigil, then leaned in and whispered something to it. It glowed briefly and faded into the plaster.

"Angel?" Luce stared at her. "Have you lost your mind?"

"It's the only thing that makes sense, Luce!" she shouted, spinning away from the window. "How he got through the wards, how he killed—" she faltered, and then forged ahead. "That takes serious power, and besides, I'm pretty sure they have the market cornered on gigantic, ethereal wings."

"Then why was he after me?" Luce asked blankly. Ro shrugged and returned to her art project. He mulled that prospect over for a moment, and then began getting out of bed.

"*What do you think you're doing*?" It wasn't a screech, because that would have alerted the officials that something was wrong, but it had the same effect of freezing Luce in place.

"I can't *stay*—" he began. Ro cut him off, shoving him back into bed.

"You can't *leave*, either!" She pinned his wrists when he tried to move again. "Don't make me get the crazy cuffs, Elohim."

He settled begrudgingly, and Ro sat next to him. "Look, Luce, the hospital wants you to stay here for a couple more days, and that should give us enough time to figure out how to get you from here to my house safely. We've updated the wards, so I think if we can—"

Luce interrupted her, desperate. "I'm not going to stay locked up forever, Ro! I *can't*. The only way we can fix this—"

"Is to get rid of the problem, I know," Ro sighed. Luce threw his hands up in frustration.

"I was thinking more along the lines of leaving. If I'm not around, these...*angels*," he grimaced, the word leaving a bad taste in his mouth, "will have no reason to target you—"

"They'll kill you!" she hissed.

"Maybe they will!" he snarled back. "And maybe they won't. Maybe they want something else from me. Either way, no one else gets hurt."

Ro shook her head, flaming curls flying furiously. "No way. Not an option. You are not going off on your own on a freaking *suicide mission*."

"I'm not asking for your permission—"

"—you really think you'd be able to just—"

"—need to figure this out on my own if it's my fault—"

"—like you're the only one who has a stake—"

"—leaving whether you like it or not—"

"—just have to come with you then."

Silence.

"You *what*?" All the anger and indignation that had fuelled Luce through his rant drained, only to be replaced with crushing horror. "You—no, you can't—it's too dangerous!"

Ro lifted an eyebrow. "One—no one tells me what I can and cannot do, Lucifer Elohim. Two—it's a hell of a lot more dangerous for you than it is for me. As I recall, I already kicked this toff's arse, while you were busy getting yourself tossed into walls. If he attacks you, exactly how do you plan to defend yourself?"

He looked down sheepishly. Ro nodded sharply. "Stay here for another day. I'll check you out early the morning after, and we can head out to my dad's old bunker on the Wye River."

"Your dad has a bunker?" Luce asked, tilting his head in confusion.

"Technically, it was the British Army's, but they gave it to Dad for 'excellent service' or something, and he always joked about asking for it in case of the zombie apocalypse." She frowned suddenly. "At least, I think he was joking." She considered that for a moment, then shook herself and finished off one last sigil. "That's the last of those. Stay in here; I'll be back the day after tomorrow with everything we need. Be ready."

Luce sighed and flopped back down once his friend left, shutting the lights off behind her. He stared into the dark, heat prickling his eyes. In just a few hours, his life had changed until he was a fugitive from a man he didn't even know, for a crime he knew even less about. He clenched his hands into fists to stop their trembling and rolled onto his side. He swiped roughly at his face, ignoring the sobs clogging his throat.

It was a long time before the young man was able to fall back asleep.

Ro closed her bedroom door and slid down it, thumping onto the floor and allowing herself to break down for the first time in days. Everything was spiralling out of control. A new, *powerful* player had arrived in town and started attacking her family for no apparent reason. Her powers still hadn't settled from their maturation; they wanted to seek out the thing that dared hurt their own and obliterate it.

She had lost her normal life, probably for good. And now, she was about to leave what little she had left to look for a solution that may not exist for a problem that they didn't even understand completely.

But it's for Luce, she reminded herself fiercely. *All of it, it's always been for Luce.*

Ro closed her eyes and counted to seven, letting the pain and fear wrack through her tiny frame. When she opened her eyes and sat up, she was calm and solid, prepared to turn her life on its head.

Aunt Willow was out for the night, going over to the church with the police to see if she could find anything. For all most of the town distrusted them at times or called them crackpots and falsifiers, when something evidently supernatural happened, the people knew when to call in the experts.

The ward display a few nights ago helped as well.

Ro walked to the end of the hallway, finding the large music room her grandmother had loved. "*Having magic is all well and good, Rowan,*" she would say. "*But if you don't know how to wield it properly, it's either incredibly dangerous or incredibly useless. And music is one of the strongest ways to channel your power.*"

"Oh, Grandmother," Ro whispered to the spiders. "I wish you could be here. You would have known what to do. And you could teach me more about music and magic." She let her hand rest on the old grand piano in centre place, leaving prints in the dust. Ducking her head, she stepped into the west corner and opened up the servant's stairs. Swatting away cobwebs, Ro made her way up to the attic. An old trunk and rucksack caught her eye, tucked away under several umbrellas. She shoved her way through the mess, grinning in vicious delight when her fingers traced the enchantments etched on the sides.

Hauling the luggage to the door, she turned and surveyed the room. Books she could get from the family library, and herbs from her own stores, but Grandmother Lilly had all sorts of ancient treasures. If she was lucky, she might find a couple of weapons. Ro craned her neck, spying a bundle of cloth in the back, heaped on top of another trunk. She ducked under one of the exposed beams, shaking out the dust and sneezing. It was an old cloak. Faded blue that could have been royal once, a silver knotted clasp, silver thread woven through the wool in intricate designs—

Oh. The old thing was layered in protection magicks. No wonder it wasn't moth-eaten.

Ro hastily opened the wooden trunk, revealing dozens more clothes. Tops, trousers, skirts, dresses, cloaks, hats, shoes—even pieces of armour were scattered here and there.

"How did she even find all this stuff?" Ro breathed in wonder. She gathered up three pairs of breeches, pirate-styled shirts, and boots for herself and Luce. The style was ancient, but the clothes would serve their purpose. She laid the blue cloak on Luce's pile, choosing a forest green and gold one for herself. Running her fingers over a black silk dress embroidered with tiny black battle sigils, Ro put it on her pile before she could change her mind.

Eyeing the armour doubtfully, Ro eventually picked up two small leather jack of plates, inlaid with some sort of bronze titanium alloy. To her surprise, the weight was hardly there, and she grinned as she carefully set them with the others. She stood, groaning, and shut the trunk before turning back to head to the doorway. Ro paused as the shift in light illuminated a corner unseen from the front of the room. A large rack adorned the wall, yet another trunk underneath it. Weapons gleamed in the afternoon light.

Crossing the room quickly, Ro surveyed her choices, noting that the most modern weapon seemed to be a farmer's scythe. She selected two small daggers, two short swords, and a katana. The trunk below apparently stored accessories for the weapons. She rummaged for a moment before finding the appropriate sheaths for the blades, and grabbed two whetstones, two leather belts, and a jar of leather oil. Making her way back to the door, she picked up the clothes and carefully floated the trunk and rucksack behind her as she returned to her room.

Ro dropped the trunk and rucksack onto her bed, piling the weapons and clothes on top of them. She changed into one set of breeches, shirt, and jack of plates, belting the dagger over her waist. She put the dress, her other two outfits and two of Luce's into the trunk. Folding the other pair of trousers and shirt around the other pair of boots, she shoved them into the pack and put the other armour, belt, and dagger on top. Ro laced up her boots, pacing to get a feel for them. The Grimoires went on top of the clothes in the trunk, the katana and short swords nestled between the layers. She found the engraved wooden potion box, placing small bundles of herbs inside it as well as the phials before locking it again and putting it in the trunk.

Ro quickly snuck down to the kitchen, grabbing as many different nonperishable foods as she could find. Wrapping them in long cheesecloth, she tucked the bundle next to the clothes in the rucksack, stuffing bottles of water on the other side. Her wallet she filled with the "rainy day" money she kept in an envelope taped to the underside of her bed frame (at least a couple hundred pounds) and shoved into an extra pocket in the side of the pack.

She stood back and took a deep breath, taking inventory with her hands on her hips. This was both the most reckless stunt she'd ever pulled, and something she'd never felt surer about in her life. Now all she needed was Luce and transport.

Standing on her lawn with the rucksack slung over her shoulder and dragging the trunk behind her, Ro was at a loss for where to go next. She needed a car; a bus, train, or anything public wouldn't work. The protection charms clinked in her pocket as she turned in a circle. Her eyes landed on the driveway next door and she winced.

Gabriel was going to kill her.

Ro pulled up in front of the hospital, nervously adjusting the shrouding charm hanging from the rearview mirror as she got out. She'd stuffed the charms in various nooks and crannies of the car. There was one in the boot, one under the floor mat, one in each seat, one jammed in the ashtray, one in the glove box, and one glued to the undercarriage. It wasn't ideal, but it would do until they could reach the bunker.

Pulling open the door of the hospital, Ro tried to look as casual as she could. She wasn't breaking Luce out of the hospital; the hospital was releasing him into her custody. Now she just had to convince the hospital staff of that.

Luce was sitting up in bed, scowling at the nurse bustling around his room. Ro smirked slightly before asking for his doctor, stepping out of the way hastily when she practically sprinted out the door. Ro snorted at the amount of relief on Luce's face.

"Such a tragedy, having beautiful young women fuss over you," she drawled, handing him the rucksack. "Put the clothes on, they'll offer some measure of protection. We need to move quickly; Wales is far enough away that we'll be dangerously exposed."

"To the angels," Luce said dubiously.

She glared at him. "Get dressed. I'm not sure if it's just the one, or if all of Heaven is after us, but it doesn't really matter."

Luce snorted. "Doesn't it?"

"Not really. If one of them was able to get through the wards at home, and attack us in a *church*, we should be prepared for the worst anyway. A hoard of them might have more power—"

Luce rolled his eyes. "I don't think their power is really in question here, Ro. And isn't a group called a flock?"

"That's what you're concerned about? And will you *please* put your clothes on?"

Luce huffed and yanked out the fluffy shirt. He stared incredulously at it. "Are we going to a Renaissance Faire or something?"

"Don't ask stupid questions," she muttered, leaning out the door. "I asked for the doctor ten minutes ago, where is he?"

"You expect me to go out in public like this?" Luce made no move to put it on.

She glared at him. "Yes, I do. Seriously, where is the doctor?" Ro crossed to the window, peering out at the car-park. She ignored Luce's grumbling as he tugged on the breeches and jack of plates, clumsily tying the belt and dagger over them.

"These aren't very comfortable, you know," he grumbled.

"Comfort is hardly the point, Luce. Their job is to protect you," she muttered.

"From everything but chafing, apparently," he griped.

"Something's wrong," Ro murmured. Luce paused, and then slowly finished lacing up his boots. The last time Ro had a bad feeling, her grandmother died soon after.

"Wrong how?"

Ro didn't answer his question. She didn't have to.

The explosion rocked the building, his best friend immediately lunging for the bed. She dragged him up, hauling him out of the room and down the stairs at the back. Instead of going down the hall, they made for the fire escape.

"Wait, wait, we have to—" Luce gasped out, tearing away from Ro and stumbling over to a supply cart. "Come on, take the basics. I think there's a first aid kit on the bottom, I'll get more bandages and things."

Ro knelt and pulled out a heavy plastic box, clicking it open and grabbing the rolls of bandages from her friend. Stuffing them in as best she could, Ro grabbed a few syringes and vials of morphine, as well as another spool of surgical thread. She shrugged at Luce's sceptic expression. "Hey, you wanted to stop for modern medicine. Never say never."

She shoved the lid closed and handed it to Luce, slinging his free arm around her shoulders. They burst out of the doors and limped down the stairs to the car-park.

"Why would they blow up a building?" Luce panted. Ro shot him a curious glance. "I mean, isn't their style usually sneak in and inconspicuously deal with the target?"

Ro frowned as she helped him into the passenger seat of his brother's car. "Maybe. But I think they're getting desperate. This is their third attempt to kill us—"

"You."

She blinked at him, buckling her seat belt and turning the ignition. "What?"

He shook his head, bewildered. "The first time they made a move, it was on your house and family—"

"Which is right next to yours, maybe they made a mistake—"

"They're angels, Ro. Do you really think that's likely?"

He watched her knuckles whiten as she steered the car onto the motorway out of town. Her jaw clenched stubbornly against the threat of tears. Releasing a shaky breath, Ro refused to look at him as she answered.

"No," she whispered. "No, I don't think so. But that doesn't mean they're after me."

"Ro," Luce said, quietly, gently. "I was at the church when that bloke attacked, and the hospital just now. I'll admit that. But if he was going to strike at me, why do so as soon as you get there? He knows your power, what you can do; he's felt it. If he was after me, why wait until the most powerful person in town was there to protect me?"

She sighed and bowed her head briefly. "Luce, can we not do this now? We need to get to the Wye River, and settle in for the long haul."

He nodded quickly, leaning back in his seat. "Of course. I'm sorry."

Ro shook her head fiercely. "You have nothing to be sorry for. Let's just…put on the radio or something, yeah?"

Luce quirked his mouth into some semblance of a smile, leaning forward to tap at the presets. He wrinkled his nose at some of the stations, prompting Ro to scold him.

"Don't judge me. I have a station for every occasion," she declared. Luce barked a laugh.

"That was terrible," he grinned. Ro rolled her eyes.

"Yeah, yeah. Gabriel's going to be pissed when he gets his car back."

"You're kidding. He loves this crap; not in public, of course, but you should take a look at his iPod sometime."

"Well, then, apparently I did him a favour. Oh, I love this song!"

Luce raised an eyebrow. "'Long Long Ago' by T. H. Bayly?"

She smirked at him. "And how do you know it?"

He groaned. "When your brother plays songs on a loop because he's obsessed with them, you kind of pick it up."

Beaming, Ro turned up the volume. "So you know the lyrics? Fantastic, let's have a sing-along!"

"Let's not and say we did," Luce said immediately. She pouted at him.

"Come on, it'll be fun! *Tell me the tales that to me were so dear!*" She smacked him on the shoulder, crooning out the next lines. "*Long, long ago, long, long ago!*"

Luce sighed and reluctantly joined in, smiling helplessly in response to Ro's glee. *"Sing me the songs I delighted to hear. Long, long ago, long ago!*"

Laughter broke up the rest of the song as the two of them zoomed down the roads. The next song came on, and the one after that, and for a few moments Luce was able to forget what they were running from, or even that they were running in the first place. He couldn't remember the last time he'd had this much fun, or felt this happy. Ro met his eyes, cheeks flushed and dimpled from the huge grin she was sporting. Luce felt his stomach twist, his own smile growing wider as they kept singing.

They found the bunker a few hours later.

Chapter Six

Luce glanced up from the couch as Ro trudged in. She dropped the wooden bowl that she had filled with questionable spell ingredients onto the table with a clatter and flopped down next to him.

"That's all the wards done, finally. Now we just need to find beds and a room for research, and we should be set." Ro heaved herself up with a sigh. Luce quickly sat forward.

"I can help—" he started.

Ro cut him off with a glare. "You can rest," she told him sternly, jabbing a finger in his face. "The last thing we need is you keeling over from exhaustion or the after effects of a concussion. I'll find you something better than a couch from the forties, and then try and get as organized as possible." Catching Luce's obstinate face, she wavered and then amended her decision. "Here's the deal: I wait to go exploring, on the condition that you rest as long as possible. A full eight hours of sleep, Luce, I mean it."

He grinned and hugged her, ignoring her exasperated fondness. "Thanks, Ro," he murmured, breathing in her woodsy scent. She softened slightly in his arms, before shoving him off the couch.

"To bed with you," she ordered playfully. "I'll protect you from the big bad shadows."

He rolled his eyes. "You're going to be my night-light?" he teased, walking through one of the hallways they hadn't had a chance to explore yet.

An odd expression crossed her face, amusement mostly gone. "When everything else seems lost, Luce, I will always be your light in the dark, I promise you."

He stared at her for a long moment. "Okay…thanks." He paused, a cheeky smirk curling his lips. "Do you really glow, like a fairy?"

She sniffed in mock offence. "Please, as if I could ever be a fairy. They are far too obsessed with themselves to care about humans."

Luce blinked. "Wait, fairies are real?"

Ro shrugged. "Sort of. The Fae are actually vicious little buggers, warriors more than anything. No one has seen a Fae in this dimension in ages, and they really don't like humans. They supposedly tolerate Wiccans a little more though; I think one of my ancestors saved the life of a Fae, but I never paid much attention to that story."

"Of course you didn't. Hey, look, barracks." The room only had a couple beds, but it was a communal room as well, judging by the large table and armchairs.

"I think these are CO and XO quarters, actually," Ro mused, testing one of the beds.

"CO…commanding officer. What's the XO?"

"Executive officer: the second in command. They'd usually bunk together, go over plans before revealing them to the troops. Huge bundle of laughs," she deadpanned.

Luce snorted and thumped down on the other bed. "Yeah, I'm sure. You know, you should probably sleep as well."

"I need to—"

"You need sleep Ro. Stop taking care of everything for once. The place is warded, no one knows where we are, and we're as safe as we can manage at the moment. But we'll be worse off if you run yourself into the ground. We both need to be at our best, and I need you to be at 100%. Okay?" He waited for her reluctant nod before lying down and tugging the covers over himself. "Good, now sleep. I'm beat."

"Good night, Luce," she said quietly, turning off the light before climbing under the covers herself. Listening to each other's breathing, they both drifted into dreams.

"What do you mean, he's *gone*?" Gabriel yelled at the poor doctor.

"Mr. Elohim—" the woman tried.

"Don't 'Mr. Elohim' me!" he raged. Kali squeezed his shoulder and Carmen grabbed his hand. "The hospital is in ruins, and you're telling me you've lost my brother and sister! Remind me again why, exactly, I should remain calm?"

"Because you're not helping matters by terrorizing the staff, Gabriel," Kali said tartly. "Now, leave the doctor to her work and listen to what Anthony has discovered from the police."

Gabe watched the doc scamper off before turning to his parents, jaw tight. "Well?"

Anthony gave him a disapproving look, but complied. "It was definitely intentional. Some of the patrons in the car-park saw a man with a briefcase walk in minutes before the explosion. No one can find him either, but from witness reports, the description matches the man who attacked Rowan and Lucifer before in the church; he also may have been the same man who murdered Mrs. Fitzgerald. They have put an APW out nationwide, and they have forensics looking for the source of the explosion."

"They won't find anything," Willow said, appearing on Kali's left. "That thing is clever and powerful enough that no one will find it if it doesn't want to be found. Besides, that...bomb, for lack of a better word, was in no way natural. What I do know is that Rowan will take care of Luce, and he of her. They're smart, and resourceful, and know, if not exactly what to do, then what to avoid doing. They'll be fine," she said, smiling wanly.

Gabe nodded, unconvinced. Willow's dark eyes were bagged and bloodshot, her mouth and forehead constantly scrunched up, and she had pulled her greying hair back into a messy ponytail, unbrushed. She didn't believe her words any more than they did.

A sudden thought punched all the air out of Gabe's lungs. "What are we going to tell Michael and Raphael?"

Luce wandered into the main room the next morning, rubbing his bleary eyes as he followed the smell of tea. Ro glanced up at him and gestured to the table, setting a mug and a packet of deer jerky in front of him.

"What's with the venison?" he mumbled, tearing off a piece and trying to chew it. It almost broke his jaw.

"It lasts a long time, and I found some in the storage pantry. We have other food, but I'd rather eat the old food first," she said, putting her own plate together.

"Mm," he agreed, letting the bite soften in his mouth before trying to chew it again. It gave a little easier this time.

"We're in hunting country as well, and the property for about three kilometres in any direction belongs to my family. We can catch another deer and get food that way, if necessary."

Luce raised an eyebrow. "Do you know how to prepare food from a deer? For that matter, do you even know how to hunt?"

"My dad used to take me hunting up here when I was little, before my mom died. I never actually made food from deer meat, but I watched him do it. How hard can it be?" She went over to the trunk, pulling out several books and the Grimoires. "I found a study, by the way, and there are some books there, too."

He frowned. "Your dad had books on the supernatural?"

She frowned too. "I know, it's weird. He never showed any inclination that he knew anything beyond what my mom told him, or even that he was interested in this stuff. But that room is filled to the brim with knowledge; I think there might even be texts that my mother's family never had."

"So, what, he secretly collected everything he could find on the subject? Or—" His stomach lurched as a horrible thought struck him. "Do you think the military is doing this? Some secret operation to track down and experiment on supernatural creatures? Maybe that's what Porton Down is for. It's not a military research facility, it's a supernatural one. Can they find us here? Are they going to capture us and dissect—?"

Ro was laughing.

"What?" he asked, bewildered.

"Luce," she gasped, still giggling. "I don't think the military cares about us, and if they did have a branch for supernatural creatures, there's no way Wiccans wouldn't know. Humans have a hard time fighting monsters all on their own; they would have asked for our help, or at the very least our advice. And Porton Down is for military advancement research. So advanced that the tests people have seen seem like alien activity, especially because their methods are…unorthodox." She grinned at him, eyes light and dancing.

He pouted. "Oh. Well then, that's one less thing to worry about. Now to tackle the problem of laundry."

Ro broke down in giggles again, Luce joining her a few seconds later.

"Come on, you idiot. Let's go look at books," she teased, leading the way through the twisting hallways. Luce shook his head fondly, following her.

Chapter Seven

Luce slammed the book shut, yanking another one towards him petulantly. Ro glared at him from the other end of the table.

"We've been at this for almost two months, Ro," he snapped. "What do you expect to find here that we couldn't at home?"

Hurt flashed in her eyes before they hardened. "Maybe a little hope? Or maybe a little cooperation from the one person here with me! You think you're the only one getting tired of this? I have no clue what I'm doing, Luce, same as you. Try to keep that in mind as you complain constantly, yeah?"

She stood abruptly, stalking out of the room with an armful of texts. Luce groaned and let his head fall forward into his hands. They were so screwed. He sighed and opened the book, propping up his chin with his palm, elbow on the table. His head kept nodding, eyelids slipping shut. Luce tried to stay awake, but sleep eventually dragged him under, eyes darting restlessly beneath their lids. His dreams had been getting worse, and this one was no exception.

Luce landed hard, hands and knees braced against charred ground. Another form thudded down a little ways away from him, recuperating faster than he was. The other rose, striding towards him on long legs. Luce squinted up at the blurry face, glimpsing the moving mouth but unable to hear anything past the ringing in his ears.

*The man—*angel, *Luce corrected himself as two pairs of gigantic rusty-red wings mantled threateningly—gripped his upper arm and* *hauled him upwards. Facing the creature, Luce could see a little more clearly, catching sight of pale skin and white-blond hair. But it was the eyes that held him. A startling red—almost albino, if angels could be albino, which was a stupid question considering there was an angel attacking him at the moment, and it was very much albino (did he have a concussion? Probably; he hit the ground pretty hard)—they blazed with literal fire; loathing, disgust, and disappointment lurked in their depths.*

Luce belatedly tried to get away from the angel, but was held fast by preternatural strength. It sneered and tossed him to the ground, standing over him with its hand outstretched.

A tugging came from Luce's chest, growing more intense with every passing second. It felt as if this thing was trying to rip out his heart with its mind. Which he very well may be, *Luce realized. Except his heart, apart from beating faster with adrenalin, was working just fine. This was something else, something other of his that this creature wanted to take from him.*

It yanked, hard, and Luce let out a short scream. He didn't notice the angel's head whipping around, or its hasty retreat with panic written all over its face. He did notice the sudden lack of pain, and sat up, lightheaded. He needed to find his brothers.

Luce jerked awake, elbow slipping off the edge of the table and sending his face crashing down into a book. He winced and rubbed it, trying to clear the signs of the nightmare from his face. He leaned back in his chair—and found Ro looming over him.

"When were you going to tell me about the nightmares?" She was pissed.

"It's no big deal, Ro," he protested wearily.

"Clearly it is! You've been getting lots of sleep lately, it just hasn't been restful. And now you fall asleep in the middle of the afternoon, only to have another one!" Ro took a deep breath, pain in the thin line of her mouth. "Luce, I can't help you if you don't tell me what's wrong."

"They're just nightmares, Ro," he snapped at her. "You know what they say about the subconscious working things out in your dreams. Maybe I'm finding a solution with my nightmares. It's nothing."

"It's always something, Luce," Ro said quietly. "With us, it's never just a dream. I can give you something for it—"

"I don't need your help!" He flung back his chair and stormed from the room, not missing Ro's flinch at his outburst. Already, he felt the stirrings of guilt, but he couldn't go back. Right now, he needed to be alone.

Ro massaged her temples, wishing for the times when she and Luce had been able to just talk to each other. Now it seemed as if all they did was push each other's buttons.

She dragged another tome across the table, opening it with a distinct lack of optimism. They were quickly running out of resources, even with the fresh material the bunker had. Not that she was telling Luce that. He had enough to worry about, especially now that his nightmares were getting worse.

The rest of the afternoon Ro spent looking through her grandmother's Grimoire and filling out her own. They needed to explore the rest of the bunker at some point, but until they exhausted their research she refused to accept the bunker as a long term place to stay.

By the time she returned to their room, Luce was facing away from her and buried under covers. Ro felt a surge of guilt at making him go through this, especially since the angels were apparently after her this entire time. She resolved to talk to Luce in the morning; once they got rid of whatever tension was between them, they could go back to being the amazing team she knew they were.

She leaned over and turned off the light, casting one last glance at her best friend before shutting her eyes and fading out of consciousness.

Minutes later, Ro woke to Luce yelling and seizing for the second time in as many months. She leapt out of bed and on top of him, pinning him in place with her hips and clamping his arms to the mattress.

"Luce, calm down, wake up, please, you're fine, you're safe, I'm here, it's okay, please, please please just *wake up*—"

He gasped awake, immediately stilling as he stared up at her. Distantly, she noted their awkward position, but right now was too relieved to care much. Ro released his arms and wrapped around him instead, burying her face in his neck and shaking as he hugged her back.

"What happened?" Luce eventually asked through the hair in his mouth. He didn't have the heart to dislodge her when she was clinging to him like this. She shook her head, not moving. He sighed lightly. "Ro, I've been having nightmares for weeks, and I know you've noticed before yesterday. What was so different about this time?"

"It was like the church all over again," she whispered. "You were seizing and shouting and not waking up, and there's no help for miles around, and I couldn't do anything—"

"You did," Luce said softly. "You grounded me, let me come back to myself. It's been getting worse, yeah, but this was…realer somehow. Like the night—"

He broke off, prompting Ro to raise her head and look at him. "The night what, Luce?"

He stared back at her for a long moment, searching for something in her champagne-gold eyes. When he finally spoke, his words were heavy and measured, designed to keep her calm. "The last time the dream was this intense, that thing showed up at your house, Ro. If he finds us…" Luce didn't have to finish the sentence for her to understand his meaning. They both knew what would happen if the angels tracked them down. Or at least, they had an idea.

"They won't," she said, trying to instil confidence into her voice. It didn't help, considering she was still shaken up by Luce's…episode. "The place is warded from top to bottom, if we have to go out for food or supplies we have weapons and protective clothing, as well as amulets. We are as safe as we can be right now, Luce. We just have to hold out—"

"Until what, Ro?" Luce interrupted wearily. "Until we find a solution? That's not going to happen anytime soon, we both know that, not without a miracle—and something makes me think those aren't going to head our way anytime soon either. Until help arrives? Help from where? We are trapped here, with no other options, and unless God Himself shows up—why are you staring at me?"

"Lucifer," Ro breathed, awed. "You are a genius."

"Yes," he agreed immediately. "What about, exactly?"

"God. Or pagans. Hey, I'll settle for aliens at this point. If we can find someone with greater power and influence on our side, our chances of fighting back—successfully, mind you—increase exponentially." She jumped up, dragging him with her. "Come on, I think there's a chapter in Grandmother's Grimoire about the different pagans and how to summon them. If you can find a Bible here, we might be able to use that as well."

Luce couldn't help but smile wanly at Ro as she tugged him down the hallway. Abruptly, she turned into the kitchen, letting go of his hand and making a beeline for the cabinets. Rummaging for a minute, she pulled out a packet of hot chocolate and two mugs, shooting an expectant look over her shoulder. He shook his head fondly, turning the hot tap on and filling the kettle.

They moved around each other easily, the routine born from countless years of sleepovers and late night visits. Whenever one of them had a hard day, or a bad dream, or if they got fed up with their own family, they would go next door and sit in the kitchen for a couple of hours. The two would drink a mug of hot chocolate—the real kind, with melted chocolate and milk—and talk of absolutely nothing.

Of course, they couldn't get milk or real chocolate in the bunker, but it was nice to have the link back home—back to happier times. Luce and Ro moved into the study, carefully cradling the cups so as not to spill on the books. Clearly neither of them was going to get any more sleep that night, so they might as well be productive.

For whatever reason, the only Bible in the bunker was in a shoebox—in the non-functioning fridge. Luce just rolled his eyes at the general weirdness of his friend's family. Ro had pulled a ton of pagan texts from…somewhere. He had no idea how she found so many different ones when they'd been running out of resources, but he guessed they just hadn't been searching for specific information before.

Luce looked across at Ro, the candlelight—they still hadn't been able to find a generator without descending into the depths of the bunker; with their luck, it was probably outside—illuminating her skin and hair. She swept it back, leaning over a particularly old tome, from the Middle Ages or something. Her brow creased as she ran a finger down its page, mouth pursed as she took notes. Luce blinked, quickly looking down.

When their lives weren't in danger and the world wasn't ending, he could figure out whatever he was feeling. Until then, he had bigger issues to worry about.

Several hours later, they had nothing to show for the 'breakthrough.' Pagans, like most religious figures, worked off of a 'faith base.' All their power came from humans and the belief in the deities' power, which in turn created the humans. And all religions coexisted, apparently. At least, according to Ro. Luce was going to assume she mostly knew what she was talking about and just go with it.

If he thought about it too hard, his head threatened to split open. Again.

The point was, as Ro explained to him dejectedly, that while each pagan still had some followers, Christianity was so influential and widespread that their power was exponentially amplified compared to other religions. Even if Ro managed to convince every pagan in existence to fight the Judeo-Christian angels with them, Heaven would still be ridiculously stronger.

God appeared to be their only hope, because Luce didn't think the aliens really cared, and even if they did, neither he nor Ro knew how to contact them. Of course, that hadn't stopped Ro from trying anyway. Well, it was that or she was finally interior decorating, but the alien theory was more likely.

Luce was currently getting lunch for Ro, because she had immersed herself in nearly a metre of paper and didn't look like she was surfacing any time soon. He frowned down at the plate of venison, stomach clenching in dread at eating the shite *yet again*. It was new and interesting at first, but he might actually throw up soon if he didn't get any variety in his diet.

Still, unless he wanted to risk getting killed or captured or whatever Heaven wanted to do with them for the sake of going to the supermarket a few miles outside of the property, venison was the main meal. Ro had at least had the foresight to bring extra food.

"Ro, I'm going to check out the hunting prospects, okay?" Luce set the plate down at her elbow, getting only a hum of acknowledgement in return. He rolled his eyes and left her to it, scribbling a short note and sticking it in one of the texts closest to Ro. She would get it sooner or later. Hopefully sooner, so if he ran into trouble she'd know where to start.

Of course, if she got his note and decided to murder him because of it, then the note would hurt him rather than help, but he'd take his chances. Luce dug around in the trunk Ro brought with them and shoved in their room the first day here. He put the shirt and breeches he'd worn in the hospital back on with a grimace. He laced up the boots and armour, wrapping the cloak around his shoulders and pulling the hood over his head.

Luce felt stupid wearing all the layers of period clothing, but Ro was convinced it would protect him. He wasn't exactly a magic guru, so he usually ended up trusting Ro's word on these things. He grabbed a crossbow from an armoury down the hall—he didn't even want to know why the military had crossbows as well as their more…modern weapons—and hoped he could remember how to use it well enough to hunt.

His…Anthony had taken the brothers on a hunting trip once or twice before. Luce had never felt comfortable calling Kali and her husband his parents formally, much less casually. Despite encouragement from his brothers and…carers, Luce barely acknowledged his adopted family to their face, much less in his head. His brothers, Ro and the rest of the Fitzgeralds, and Carmen were always enough for him.

Luce slipped silently out of the bunker, lengthening his stride and keeping his weight on his toes. Luce may not have been as quick as Michael or as quiet as Gabriel, but he wasn't exactly useless. He glanced around, taking in trails of prints and broken vegetation. Wales didn't lack in wildlife, and anything that crossed into the bunker's property was legal for him to hunt.

He followed a set of particularly fresh prints, looking like three or four deer. He would have preferred something else, but at least with fresh meat and whatever wild vegetables he could scrounge up out here they could maybe improvise with stew or a pie. The tracks led to a small clearing walled by rocky cliffs. If he was a deer, he wouldn't lead himself and his family into a death trap, but to each his own.

The stag clearly had a notion of how stupid this plan had been, because he was standing guard as the doe and fawn ate their fill. Luce deliberated for a moment before taking careful aim at the male. He only had a few arrows and not a lot of time, so he couldn't waste his shots. Pulling the trigger, the shaft thudded through the stag's throat as the fawn and doe took off. Luce quickly reloaded and aimed for the heart next, unable to get a clear shot at the skull as the deer flailed and tossed his head.

He finally died, and Luce breathed a quick sigh of relief before clambering down into the clearing. He would have to lug the carcass back to the bunker before doing anything else. They would probably take the meat and skin, at the most, and throw everything else out for the wolves.

There were wolves in Wales, right? He frowned, and then shrugged. Some kind of predator would get the leftovers. Circle of life, and all that.

He cast around for vines or something that he could use to move the deer, slumping when he found none. Apparently, Luce was going to carry the thing on his shoulders. Next time, he was bringing rope.

Luce paused as he realized what he just admitted, if only to himself. He was accepting his and Ro's predicament as long term; he was settling in. Luce scowled and heaved the body over his shoulders, clamping the legs to his chest in an effort to keep it still. He turned to make his way out of the clearing—

And froze, staring at the figure standing on top of the wall across from him. It wasn't the same bloke as before—this man was Korean for reasons best known to himself—but he had that same *presence* as the other one, the same taste of power tingling in the air. Luce didn't breathe, terrified that any moment the angel would leap down and smite him.

That was what they did, right? The angels? Come down from on high and smite the evil and wrongdoers and their enemies?

Except this one evidently hadn't got the memo, because he hadn't made any move towards him, and was still looking around curiously. There were a couple times his eyes passed right over Luce, and he didn't seem all that bothered Luce was there. In fact, as Luce slowly shifted his weight in the direction of the path, the angel didn't seem to realize a living, breathing teenage boy was right there in front of him.

Asian Angel frowned, lifted a hand, and pushed at the air. He was repelled violently backwards with a flash of blue sparks, crashing into a tree.

Well, that answered that question. Now Luce just had to figure out whether the boundary extended all around them or was just in the one place so he didn't accidentally reveal himself.

"*Lucifer!*" The furious hissing didn't actually register as his name for a few seconds; he thought a snake was upset about its dinner or something. But no, it was Ro, and she was pissed.

"What do you think you're doing?" She didn't raise her voice, glancing fearfully at the prone angel.

"Getting dinner?" Luce offered dubiously. Ro blinked, as if she had only just now noticed the giant stag Luce had draped around his shoulders. And now that he was paying attention to it as well, his back decided it had had quite enough of that, thank you very much. "And, *ow*, it hurts, so do you think you could give me a hand here?"

She smirked and raised an eyebrow before waving a hand at him. He opened his mouth, annoyed, before the weight lifted off his back and the deer floated docilely beside them. Luce stared for a moment, and then made his way out of the clearing, shaking his head. Ro cast one last glance at the clearing where the angel—who had disappeared by now, of course—had stood before following Luce back to the bunker.

Chapter Eight

Luce woke screaming that night.

At least he wasn't seizing again; Ro had to appreciate the small things.

She was not appreciating Luce's attitude, though.

"Just try it, Luce! It might actually do you some good!" Ro yelled at him. His face set stubbornly. She threw her hands into the air and set the bottle down on the table with a hard clack.

"When you change your mind, come find me," she snapped. Stepping out of the room, Ro automatically turned towards the library. She glanced back at the doorway before heading down the hallway, deeper into the unexplored parts of the bunker. This was as good a time as any to find out about where they would be staying for the foreseeable future. The normal, human prediction kind, not the premonition and scrying kind.

Most of the rooms appeared to be empty but for five centimetres of dust. If the place had any cockroaches, they'd probably died too. Or left for greener pastures. There was a stairway at the end of the corridor, and she decided to head down. Who knows, she might find the generator down here.

There wasn't a generator on the first floor down. There was a football pitch, though. Or, well, it was a pitch-sized room, though she didn't see the purpose of it at first. She stepped forward—and the room came alive.

Not literally, thank the stars, because she would have had to exorcise it. But clearly it was a training room, and whatever it was programmed to do obviously had enough energy to do so. Or it was a booby trap.

Their fridge needed more motivation.

The training room/booby trap took up the entire floor, so Ro continued down the stairs. The next floor wasn't quite as large, but it was still a decent size, and the only room on it appeared to be a target range. Archery, guns—there was even a *rocket launcher* in one corner.

Three floors below the main one, Ro found the generator. Unfortunately, she had no idea how to fix whatever was broken. She didn't even know if this one was broken, but until she could figure it out, Ro wasn't planning on turning it on and potentially blowing up Britain.

She wished Carmen and the rest of the Elohims were here, and not for the first time. Carmen, while more apt at virtual programming, still knew the most about technology out of all of them. Michael was a brilliant strategist, Raphael probably knew how to handle Luce's nightmares better than her—he was always the better healer—and Gabriel was a fountain of weird trivia and surprisingly useful advice. They had always worked together to solve problems, and now they only had a third of the group.

Ro wanted her family back to the way it had been before all this started. She wanted it to be summer break again, when Grandmother Lilly was still alive and the biggest worry was which university they'd get into.

Stars above, would they even be able to go to university now? They'd missed tons of school, and that was the tiniest factor. If they were ever able to leave the bunker, Ro didn't think they could do something as normal as *university*. She slid down the wall and stared at the hulk of metal and gears.

Luce found her like that.

He sat down beside her, not saying anything. She leaned over and rested her head on his shoulder. Luce lifted an arm and pulled her closer. Ro breathed in his familiar scent, taking comfort in pine and cinnamon and snow.

"What are we doing, Luce?" she whispered. His hand tightened on her shoulder.

"We're doing what we can," he replied. "We're surviving, and fighting, and trying our best. It's all anyone can do, Ro, especially in our situation."

"I'm pretty sure our situation is unique."

"Maybe," he agreed easily. "But it makes it that much harder for people to judge us."

"Who's going to judge us?" Ro twisted to look at Luce incredulously. "The dust mites? Unless you're planning on telling a normal person what we've been through for the past months, no one else is going to know, Luce, much less judge."

He frowned down at her. "I don't want to get locked up in the loony bin any more than you do—" Luce tilted his head, considering. "You don't want to be locked up in the loony bin, right?" She smacked his chest, laughing along with him. "Seriously, Ro, I'm not saying we go around talking about how we are on Heaven's hit list. I'm saying that given the problems we have to deal with, we are doing remarkably well. *You* are doing *amazing*."

Ro grinned. "You're not so bad yourself, Luce. You don't give yourself enough credit."

Luce rolled his eyes. "Out of the two of us, which one is the insanely powerful Wiccan?"

"Hey, you never know," Ro teased. "Maybe you could manifest if you tried really hard."

He snorted, "Yeah, I don't think that's going to happen. Not unless you rubbed off on me or something."

"It doesn't work like that," she said, getting to her feet. "Come on, there are more stairs, which means more floors, which means...probably more training stuff. Did you see the football field?" She glanced back at him.

"The one that tried to kill me when I stuck my head in the door to look for you?" Luce said dryly. "Yeah, I caught a glimpse."

"Someone's sassy today," she snarked back. "I found a rocket launcher in the range, and the generator is on this floor—I have no idea why it's so large, unless this thing goes to the centre of the earth—so maybe there will be something a little…different…" She trailed off in awe, staring into the room.

"I've lost you, haven't I?" Luce asked, looking at her in amusement. She moved forward slowly, paying him no mind. Luce nodded and sighed dramatically. "How could I possibly hope to compete with a room full of ink and paper?"

"What?" Ro wasn't even listening, wandering deeper into the aisles. Luce nodded firmly.

"I'm just going to leave you here, then," he called, already out in the stairwell. She absently waved over her shoulder.

The fifth floor was made up entirely of barracks, probably in case of nuclear fallout. Or the zombie apocalypse. The floor below was an armoury three times the size of the one on the main floor—and twice as much variety.

The final level was the real treasure.

A large laboratory stretched across the room, old beakers standing on metal tables scattered around. Large cabinets lined the walls, presumably filled with ingredients and equipment. Luce slowly wove around the room. At the back, a large bookshelf held thick leather journals, each crammed into the smallest space possible.

He tried to pull out one of the middle ones; he worked his fingers between the spine and the shelf and gradually tugged the book out, eventually latching on with both hands and yanking with his entire upper body. The book came free, along with four others. Luce picked them up and carelessly stacked them on a nearby tabletop, opening the one he had originally picked. He flipped through the pages, squinting at the scribbled notes and diagrams and formulas. Whoever wrote this was very fond of blowing things up, judging by the observations and singed paper.

This—this almost looked like a combination of magic and science, like technology and spells woven together in patterns so intricate it seemed natural. Which, Luce realized, it was. Science and magic achieved mostly the same goals, even if one was a little vaguer than the other—unless you studied alchemy for a living, apparently. On their own, wild, they probably worked better with each other than most humans on a good day.

Luce skimmed through the other books on the table. Overall, they were about how magic and science interacted, but the focus differed.

One was about organic magic—was that food or people?—and biology, chemistry, and physics; one was about elements used as ingredients instead of traditional plants; yet another discussed the advancement of magic over technology and how they could supplement each other.

He gazed at the bookshelf in awe; every volume held new discoveries, and there were more than fifty, maybe more than a hundred. The amount of knowledge collected over hundreds of years—some of the oldest tomes looked like they were made from actual parchment—would hold invaluable information. His breath caught as he realized that if the lab was any indication, the records kept in the library might have exactly what they needed to get Heaven off their backs.

He raced back up to the fourth floor, bursting in and shouting for Ro. She emerged from the shadowy depths reproachfully, several books clutched to her chest.

"All you need now are the glasses," Luce said, distracted. "I'm very impressed with your intimidating librarian imitation."

She scowled at him. "Where have you been?"

Luce lit up, recalling why he'd dashed up here. "There are a couple more floors; barracks on the next, an armoury below that, and the seventh…Ro, the seventh is a *lab*."

She rolled her eyes. "Well, that's you sorted out then. Try not to blow anything up."

He shook his head impatiently. "Ro, I found these journals in the lab. They're full of theories and observations and experiments and—"

"Science," Ro interrupted. "Your point?"

"These are scientific journals, Ro. If the books in here are half as detailed—"

"They might have a solution. Hell, I'd even settle for a clue to a solution at this point," Ro said excitedly, dumping the books in her arms onto a side table. "I found these, which are just really old Grimoires, but maybe we can find more reference texts."

Luce followed her into the next stack, craning his neck to see the top shelves. Ro pulled books out, seemingly at random, and stacked them in his arms until he could barely see over the top. And they were heavy things of leather and wood and expensive paper, instead of lightweight paperbacks or, the horror, a digital collection that could be searched.

You'd think the military would have better resources.

Chapter Nine

"Well, on the bright side, I found details on succubae and incubi mating habits that I never wanted to know," Luce said gloomily, several days later.

"How is that a bright side?" Ro asked, peering over the candles at him. Lamps were attached to the ends of each table and stack, but the generator hadn't been fixed yet. Luce wondered if there was a manual in here for it. Of course, if one of them actually tried to fix the stupid thing, it would probably blow up instantly.

"I'm expanding my horizons?" he suggested. Ro sent him a weird look.

"Expand them in other directions. I found a section on fallen angels, but so far nothing about the ones up top." She reached over and took a tome out of his stack.

"Maybe we're looking in the wrong place," he mused. "The Bible—"

"Written by humans," Ro dismissed.

He frowned at her. "Yes, I know. However, most of the information was told to the human writers by somebody, right? They didn't hack into Heaven's secret library or something."

"Heaven's secret library?" Ro looked like she was trying very hard not to laugh.

"I'm pretty sure they're archaic enough not to use computers. Pity, it would make things much easier," Luce sighed.

Ro lost it.

"It's really not that funny, Ro," he reproached. She flapped a hand at him.

He watched her, slightly disturbed. "Breathe, Ro. I hear it's good for your health."

She broke down again. Luce smiled faintly along with her.

"Oh, wow," she gasped finally, wiping her eyes and sitting back in her chair. "I can't remember the last time I laughed that hard. Thanks, Luce."

"Clearly, my sole purpose in life is to make you happy," he told her, completely serious. She just snorted and turned back to the books.

"I'm going to find more; you coming?" she asked, standing and stretching. He shook his head, flipping the pages carefully.

"I'll finish this stack off, go ahead." Ro nodded and grabbed the extra candle on the table. It moved around her like a halo, illuminating everything else she touched. Luce watched her walk off, until the shadows swallowed the light behind her. He sighed and turned back to reading.

They had a lot of work to do.

Uriel stared at the nervous soldier in front of him. Raziel favoured the Asian ethnicities over the other…varieties, for reasons best known to himself. Uriel had fashioned himself after the more traditional Caucasian appearance, so as to better blend in with the primitive, hairless apes. Not, of course, that they should have to. His unique appearance was the result of his tiny rebellious streak.

"What did you find?" Uriel kept his tone neutral, watching as Raziel gulped anxiously. Millennia of practice honed his ability to intimidate the younger, less experienced angels into doing what he wanted or spilling secrets they rather would have kept from him. The soldier shifted from one foot to the other. Uriel frowned. That was a very…*human* motion. Perhaps Raziel was getting too attached to the creatures defiling their Father's greatest creation.

"There is a place, within the United Kingdom the humans call Wales." Raziel frowned, as if the name tasted strange on his tongue. "It appears empty and unoccupied, but when I attempted to investigate further, some force obstructed my path. I believe it was Wiccan magic."

Uriel tilted his head to the side, his shrewd eyes reminiscent of a bird of prey. "At the girl's—" he sneered the word, "house, Wiccan wards activated the moment I entered. I was barely able to defend myself against the matriarch before I was ejected from the residence."

"You believe it is the same woman?" The younger angel was shocked.

Uriel scowled at the fledgling's incompetence. "No. She is dead. I believe it is her descendant, the granddaughter. The girl showed an extreme…attachment to Lucifer in his human form. If not eliminated, she could threaten the entire balance of the world."

"What do you propose we do?" Raziel asked hesitantly. Uriel glowered.

"I do not *propose* anything," he snapped. "I do what I am ordered, as will you."

"Yes, of course," the soldier soothed. "What are your orders, then?"

"Find them," he said immediately. "Find a way past the wards. We need to separate the Wiccan from the Morningstar, and help him retrieve his former glory."

"Yes, Archangel." Raziel bowed and flew off, the rest his garrison joining him as they dove off the Edge of Heaven.

Uriel smiled in satisfaction. Soon, that pesky witch would be dead, and the path to the Morningstar would be clear.

Luce hadn't been getting a lot of sleep.

Ro heard him tossing and turning in the night, long before she was able to drift off. They went to bed late as it was, but when she got up—and she didn't exactly sleep in either—Luce already had breakfast cooked and had taken a shower.

Thank the stars the water had been working when they got here, or she might have taken her chances with the divine mercenaries.

After a few days of this, and the bags under Luce's eyes steadily getting heavier, Ro decided to place a monitoring charm on his bed.

When she checked it, Ro was amazed Luce wasn't comatose from exhaustion.

"Are your nightmares worse?" she demanded first thing that morning. Luce raised an eyebrow at her and handed her a plate.

"Hello, Ro, good morning to you too. How are you?"

"I asked you first. Don't dodge the question," she snapped.

"They've been getting better," he evaded.

"Right. And is this development from actual improvement, or just the fact that you've only slept for roughly two hours a night the past week?" Ro folded her arms and glared stubbornly at him. Luce scowled back just as fiercely.

"I'm dealing. The library is very extensive, as is the lab—"

"I offered to *help* you, Luce," Ro said desperately. "You don't have to do this by yourself. Let me in, *please*."

The two just stared at each other, feeling the distance between them stretch further. Ro chuckled bitterly and broke eye contact.

"How did we get here?" she asked softly. "We used to be able to tell each other everything, do everything together. Now look at us; we can barely help each other, because we refuse to let each other in."

"You're not at fault here, Ro," Luce rebutted.

"Yes, I am," she said quietly. "I've been keeping my own secrets; I didn't want to worry you more than you already were." Ro took a deep breath. "My magic is out of control, Luce. It's volatile, and I've been practicing, but I'm scared. It feels wrong, forced, like maybe I wasn't supposed to have this power."

Luce stepped forward and wrapped his arms around her. "It's new and unfamiliar, but that doesn't mean you aren't supposed to be magic. You are the strongest and most competent Wiccan I know, and if anyone deserves this, you do." He tilted her chin, catching her gaze. "As much as you've been learning about magic your entire life, there's no one here to help you, and it's not exactly a stress free environment."

"Yeah, I know. In theory. For some reason my heart doesn't quite understand that yet." Ro wound her arms around Luce, perfectly content to bury her face in his chest.

"Anything I can do?" Luce offered.

Ro shrugged. "I'll make you a deal. You can help with my magic if you let me help with the nightmares. Want to tell me about them?"

He sighed and settled himself into one of the armchairs in the main lounge. "They aren't clear, or long, or sane. It's just…scenes of something really bad."

"Can you tell what it's about?" Ro plopped down on the sofa across from him.

"Kind of? There's lots of fighting, with blades of some kind, I think. The only other sound is wings, but I never see those. Mostly, I remember falling and burning."

Ro leaned forward suddenly, examining his face closely. Luce waited, long used to her weird habits.

"Remember from the dreams?"

He blinked, confused. "Um…maybe? It feels real, the way a memory does when you relive it in your sleep, but it might have just been something I read."

"Luce, unless the writer is intimately familiar with falling as he burns alive, I don't think you could get quite the same effect." He sighed and slumped back in the chair.

"Yeah, well, one can hope, right? A couple months after we got here, I dreamed the git that stalked and attacked us was beating me up again, except we were somewhere else, and he seemed…warier, like he thought he was going to get caught. And was scared of it." Ro watched him, brow furrowed.

"Were you in Heaven?"

He blinked. "What?"

"Do you think you were in Heaven? The fighting, the wings, the angel; there's not a lot of other possibilities left, Lucifer." She looked sad, and a little resigned. He frowned at the use of his full name. Wait—

"Michael, Raphael, Gabriel, and Lucifer Elohim," she whispered, reading his face. "Elohim means 'of God' in Hebrew. Not exactly subtle, but it gets the message across."

"So what, you think my family are the four archangels? Ro, this is out there, even for you." Luce shook his head roughly.

"Hey, I know it's coincidence and conjecture, but we are hiding from heavenly assassins. We can't really afford to rule anything out based on a crazy factor," Ro said, standing. "Now, there are a couple exercises I can try that will hopefully calm my magic down. You're going to be my focus." When he froze in sick anticipation, she hastily clarified. "You don't have to do anything but sit there and look pretty. Just don't do anything to startle me and I'll be fine."

"Look pretty?" Luce asked, deciding to be amused rather than offended. Or terrified.

"Your aura glows a nice reddish-gold, like a hearth fire. It's familiar to me, and as long as you are calm, relaxed, and relatively happy, we'll be good."

"And if I'm not?" Luce immediately wondered why he thought it was a good idea to ask that question; he probably really didn't want to know the answer.

"Then my magic will overreact to what it perceives as a threat, which won't actually exist, and blow us all up."

"And you thought this was a good idea?" Luce yelped.

"Probably not that bad," Ro amended. "But it's not going to give us warm fuzzies."

"Yeah, that's *really* not helping me stay calm."

"Stop being such a baby. Listen to the sound of the universe."

"The universe has a sound?"

"It goes *OM*."

That night, Ro handed him the same bottle she'd tried to force on him before. He just looked at it.

"It's not poison, Luce. Unless you want to call it poison for your nightmares, in which case yes, it is poison."

He moved his stare from the bottle to her.

"Just drink it, you wanker."

A hint of a smile flitted across his lips as he uncapped it and poured the liquid down his throat. Luce instantly gagged and spit out what little was in his mouth.

"What was in that stuff?"

"Do you really want to know?" Ro looked far too happy after trying to kill him.

"Not when you say it like that, I don't." He eyed her warily. "I'm not going to be dreaming of weird things, am I?"

She rolled her eyes. "You won't dream at all. If it works."

"What do you mean, *if it works*?" Luce squawked.

"Well, in theory it works, but I'm not sure if your dreams will be affected quite the same way. If they're memories, it has less effect, and external mystical forces negate it completely."

"This would have been nice to know before I drank your potion, Ro."

"Would you have done it if I did tell you?" she asked sceptically.

"Of course. If you had told me what was in it, probably not. But," he sat down on his bed, already feeling lethargic. "I want to know the chances of this actually working."

"Just think of it like an experiment," Ro suggested. "If it works, you just have a really screwed up brain. If it doesn't, then we have way bigger problems."

"Such as?"

"Could be someone's using you as a conduit, to send messages and warnings. Maybe our earlier theory was correct. Maybe it's a scare tactic by the angels—"

"The angels can hack my brain?" It was supposed to be indignant, but Luce was so tired now that it came out kind of stoned.

"Not exactly; they could be sending you the dreams, but that doesn't mean they can locate you or read your mind at a distance."

"At a distance?" He was slurring his words now.

Ro laughed gently. "In the morning, Luce. We'll go over the rest in the morning. Get some sleep, for once."

Luce murmured something; probably an important something, but he was just so *tired*…

Chapter Ten

"Less effective."

Ro looked up from the bacon, toast, and beans she'd been pushing around her plate. Luce stood across from her, arms folded, empty bottle placed very precisely on the table in front of him.

"Sorry?" she ventured.

"You said it would make the dreams less effective, Ro," Luce gritted out. "Not that they would be amplified."

She blinked. "That's because it doesn't do that. Kind of the opposite. If they are memories, it sort of detaches you from them, giving them a more dreamlike quality instead of just taking them away. If they only got stronger…"

"What?" he snapped. She raised an eyebrow. He glowered.

"Something…boosted the signal, for lack of a better word." Ro shoved a plate towards Luce, refusing to elaborate until he sat down and started eating. "By trying to block it out, whatever triggered your memories in the first place must have forced more dreams to the surface in retaliation."

"So, I am going to be suffering through these the rest of my life," he sulked, stabbing at his toast and beans. He had never liked bacon; no food should have that much grease in it.

Ro shrugged. "It depends."

"On?" Luce prompted when she didn't say anything else.

"What you need to remember, if there is an underlying message, that sort of thing."

"How long is that going to take?" he demanded.

"Depends." Luce glared. "If you fight it, could take ages for you to remember everything. If you allow it to happen naturally, it probably will still take a while. If you actively help it along, a couple weeks at most, a few days at the least."

"Help it along how?" Ro sighed and shoved her breakfast away.

"Meditation can focus the brain on what you've lost. That method will probably take a few weeks. Getting as much sleep as possible, maybe with a few potions, would last about as long. If you started writing the dreams down and making sense of them, working things out and accepting them in the real world, it will cut down on time." Ro drained her glass and put her dishes in the sink. For whatever reason, the bunker didn't believe in dishwashers.

"And the few days option?" Luce said warily. Ro probably excluded it for a reason, but he was incapable of letting issues go.

"Luce," Ro started warningly. "It's not exactly ideal, especially considering our situation. We can't afford to have you laid up in bed—"

"We can't afford to have me slipping up and making stupid mistakes because I'm exhausted and distracted!" Luce interrupted, jerking to his feet and pacing angrily. "It's better to get it over with as soon as possible, like ripping off a plaster."

"It's not exactly the same as a plaster, Luce!" Ro exploded. "This kind of magic could rip your *mind* wide open. The human brain is delicate, and if I don't do it right, this spell would overwhelm you and drive you insane. I'm not prepared to take that risk."

"Ro," Luce said quietly, trying to soothe her anger and underlying fear with his own calm certainty. "I trust you."

"Well, that makes one of us," she said bitterly. "I don't trust my magic; I can barely trust myself with mundane problems. Luce, I can't do this."

He took her hands, refusing to let her pull away. "Yes, you can," he told her firmly.

Ro choked on a laugh. It kind of made him want to cry. "How can you possibly be so *sure*?" She looked up at him desperately, and he saw the strain, the fear, the hell this was putting her through. Luce tugged her to him and hugged her, kissing her hair softly.

"Because I know you, Ro. You have never stopped fighting, never let anything beat you—unless it's Gabriel and you're going easy on him when you're debating or playing chess—and you have *always* had my back." He drew back slightly to catch her eyes. "You've never let me down, never let me be hurt if you could help it. There is no one I would trust more with my mind and with my life."

She stared at him, dumbstruck. He didn't look away, needing her to understand that he was completely serious. Ro let out a wet snort, scrubbing at her cheeks with the heels of her palms.

"Wow, you really know how to make a girl feel special, Luce," she tried.

Luce shook his head. "You are special. And I'm not sugar-coating anything or giving you false hopes and assurances. You are the most brilliant woman I know, and one of the bravest."

"That is a nice way of saying I'm stubborn beyond belief."

"It's the *truth*. You are stubborn, yes, but that is what lets you be brave and brilliant."

Ro watched him carefully, looking at him in that piercing way of hers that made Luce feel like she was reading his mind.

"You aren't reading my mind right now, are you?" he asked suspiciously.

Ro blinked and laughed. "I don't need to be a mind reader to know what you're thinking, Luce. People are surprisingly open with their expressions, and I've known you far too long."

"Well, that's comforting," Luce deadpanned. She rolled her eyes and made her way to the study. Her Grimoire was open on the table, still being filled in. It would probably still be unfinished when…when Ro could no longer research.

"I think I have a spell in here…" Ro muttered. "If it's not in here, it'll be in Lilly's."

"Lilly?" Ro never called her grandmother by her first name.

"When a student talks about their mentor in the context of studies, it's inappropriate to call them by familiar names or recognize a personal relationship with them," Ro said. She made a little noise of triumph and held the book up. "Got it. It'll take me a while to set it up, and I'll have to change it to your situation, but your problem should be over by the end of the week."

Luce hummed. "I can't even remember which month it is, let alone the day of the week."

Ro's movements slowed. "How long have we been here?"

They looked at each other blankly. "Guess we'll worry about that later. We might want to call our families, though," Luce suggested.

"Yeah, probably. We're getting your head sorted out first," Ro added sternly. Luce held up his hands in supplication.

"Do you see me arguing? I'll do what I can, if you need help." He watched her clear a space in the middle of the lounge, shoving the rugs and chairs up against the far wall.

"Your lab has tons of stuff, right? I need you to get these things. If they aren't in the lab, they might be outside or in the kitchen." Ro handed him a list and spun around in the centre of the room. Luce stared at her.

"Okay, then. Anything else?"

"I need chalk," Ro murmured, apparently to herself as she disappeared back into the study. Luce shrugged and made his way downstairs, reading the list as he went.

"What kind of spell is she using?" Luce asked the air, staring at the ingredients in disbelief. "Rosemary, eyebright, dandelion, caraway, cloves, lavender; does she want to open an interdimensional tea shop on the side or something?"

Luckily, the stores of dried herbs weren't too damaged or depleted, and he was able to find most of the plants. Eyebright had been a little difficult until he realised that, the previous tenants being old scientific people (probably), it would be labelled as euphrasia. Caraway, however, was apparently too obscure for the military, even the more scientific side of it.

"Ro, I can't find any caraway," he called, stopping short at the sight of the room.

A large pentagram was drawn on the floor, presumably in chalk. More sigils spiralled out from the centre, leading to each of the walls. Luce walked to Ro's side, careful not to smudge any of the marks. He watched her finish the last one before speaking again.

"I could go over to the town, see if they have any there," Luce suggested. Ro turned and tilted her head, confused.

"To get the caraway," he said slowly. Her expression cleared.

"You sure you'll be okay?" she asked. "I could go instead."

"I'll be fine, Ro," he assured her, amused. "Besides, don't you need special talents to make the rest of the spell work?"

"Not really. It's making tea and then I chant a few times and then you sleep while your memories come back to you. Can you make tea?" She looked at Luce expectantly.

"Yes, but—"

"Good, brew the rosemary, lavender, and dandelion together into tea. Grind the eyebright into dust and add one tablespoon of water to make a paste. There are bowls in the cabinet; place the cloves in one and put it on the Fire point of the pentagram—" She broke off at his perplexed expression. "The Spirit point is facing the entrance door. Counter-clockwise, the next point is Air—put an empty bowl there for the caraway—then Earth, then Fire, and then Water; here's my list of the elements and their respective plants. Got it?" Ro waited for his nod before continuing. "Drink the tea, and make the paste at the end so it doesn't dry out. I'll try to be back soon, and find matches or something for the burning." Ro spun on her heel, Luce blinking rapidly behind her.

"*Burning*?"

"Any trouble?" Luce asked an hour or so later. Ro shook her head and closed the door behind her.

"Didn't see any angels, didn't feel any angels, and no one followed me. Apart from the owner of the spice shop seriously needing a personality transplant, we're golden."

"Maybe he needs a caffeine injection," Luce offered. Ro rolled her eyes.

"Whatever, it's not our problem. Did you do everything?"

"Yup. But before I give you flammable materials," he added, holding the matches out of Ro's reach when she tried to grab them, "I need to know you aren't going to do anything crazy."

"Crazier than performing a memory spell on you because I think you are the archangel Lucifer?"

He shot her a look. She crossed her arms and stared back stubbornly.

"Are you going to burn me, yourself, or any living creatures alive? Are you going to burn the bunker down?"

Ro gave him a deeply insulted glare. "It's for the incense, you prat."

"Oh," he said sheepishly, handing her the matchbook.

"Where's the paste?" she asked, putting the caraway in the empty bowl. She lit the match and dropped it on the dry herb, leaning back as it roared up.

"Here," he said, moving back from the kitchen with another bowl in his hands. "And yes, I drank the tea."

"Good." She waved him into the centre of the pentagram. "Sit Indian style." A pause. "Criss-cross applesauce, Luci."

"I am not a kindergartner," Luce gritted out. Ro smirked.

"Close your eyes and smear the eyebright on the lids. Cover them completely, and do not, under any circumstances, open them until I say it's safe. Got it?"

Luce did as she told him nervously. "Ro, exactly how dangerous is this ritual?"

She sighed. "Luce, I explained that this was unbelievably dangerous, even when done by a Lord or Lady of the Craft, before we started. If you want to back out—"

"That's not what I'm asking, Ro," he cut in, exasperated. "I just want to know the consequences, so I don't screw everything up."

Silence for a moment. "If you, at any point during the spell, throw off the balance or distract me or disturb the energies or the pentagram or do not meet the requirements dictated, the results will be catastrophic. This is huge, powerful, *wild* magic, and if gets loose, if I can't control it, it will destroy anything in its path until it burns out. It will rip your mind apart, and likely mine as well. Possibly level Snowdonia, or sink at least the whole of South Wales."

Luce let out a shaky breath. "Okay then. So, sit perfectly still, don't open my eyes, and don't breathe?"

"You can *breathe*, Luce, it's not that bad. Just...take shallow breaths."

"Great. Can we start?"

The loud crackle of flames started behind him, and Luce fought against the instinct to jump. "Now wc can. Don't speak from here on out, and for the love of the stars do not panic."

Her next words, spoken in a half-familiar dialect, seemed to come from everywhere, as if the whole world was speaking, not just Ro. The sound reverberated throughout his entire body, shaking him apart until he felt like he wasn't attached to it anymore.

...Maybe because he wasn't. He could suddenly see the room again, and tried to close his eyes. Nothing happened. He looked down...at himself. He was *floating above his body.*

Ro didn't notice that anything was out of the ordinary, or she didn't care. Or it was supposed to happen. Either way, she kept chanting.

The room started to blur, and Luce...did something to twist around. Could he twist if he didn't have a body? The bunker faded and was replaced by the same place in his dreams. Unlike then, however, this was pristine. *Luce soared over the landscape towards a city, pulled forward by whatever force the spell had over him. The tiers grew steadily more extravagant; courtyards with plants and trees he'd never seen, picturesque villas, cobblestone roads with people riding horses—or flying apparently, as one nearly buzzed him. The entire thing was perfect. Too perfect. It kind of creeped him out.*

At the centre, huge walls climbed into the air, glimmering with light from an unseen source. The castle—though it more closely resembled one of the ancient Mayan temples—was clearly the hub of the city, wherever he was. More people flew around it, ghostly shapes of wings spread out behind them. Though they were more corporeal than the shadows Ro must have seen in the church (and how did he even know that? She'd never gone into detail...), Luce still could only see the faint outline of feathers instead of solid appendages he knew they were.

Luce drifted closer to the ground, one of four colossal gates made of mother-of-pearl looming before him. Still, they couldn't block him, and he was in the Hub moments later.

It was completely hollow inside, no extra or adjoining rooms. A large pyramid rose from the middle, topped by a pedestal. Four pillars stood in each corner, inscribed with the same kind of sigils Ro had warded the hospital room with. Murals and tapestries covered the walls, each depicting a different story.

Ro would love this place, *Luce thought, before his attention was brought to the base of the pyramid. The same angel that had attacked him, both in his dreams and reality, stood there, seemingly waiting for something—or someone.*

A soft crackle, like a release of static electricity, came from behind him. He turned just in time to catch a glimpse of himself, *before the lookalike walked through him.*

Yeah, that was normal.

"What are you doing here, Uriel?" The lookalike's tone was soft, deadly in a way that made Luce want to hide behind one of the pillars, even though he apparently wasn't really here and the angel that looked so much like him couldn't hurt him.

"I needed to speak with you," the angel—Uriel, it was nice to finally put a name to the face that was hunting him and Ro—began nervously. He was scared too.

"Then you should have called me, instead of coming here. You know this place is sacred, only the archangels and our Father are allowed here—"

"There are special cases, and I needed to speak with you immediately," Uriel pleaded. "Please, Lucifer, just hear me out. Destruction threatens Heaven."

Luce gasped, dizzy at the similarities between himself and the archangel. Was this what Ro meant, when she told him her theory for the first time?

"Destruction threatens everything. Death comes to all things, eventually." Lucifer walked towards the pillar to the right of the gate they had come through, laying a hand on it and praying. Since Lucifer wasn't saying a word, Luce wasn't quite sure how he knew that either. Uriel, at least, seemed to understand that if he interrupted this ritual Lucifer would lose all patience with him.

"This is a more immediate death, an unnatural one. Death comes to all things, yes, but only when their time has come. This is not that time."

"Uriel," Lucifer turned back to the lower angel. "I appreciate your concern, but if Heaven was threatened, do you not think the archangels would know of it? That our Father would not know?" He shook his head. "Go back to your garrison, Uriel."

"There are some things Father does not see," Uriel said quietly. The other two went very, very still.

"That is extremely close to blasphemy, little brother," Luce rebuked. "Our Father is everything; he sees all and knows all."

"Then perhaps he has not deigned to share it with any other but himself?" Uriel ventured.

"What do you fear threatens us, Uriel? What has you so worried that you risk going against our family and everything we stand for?"

Uriel fixed his gaze on the floor, clearly not brave enough to meet the older being's eyes. "The humans. They have the gift of free will, and I fear this will have consequences that no one, not even our Father could predict. The ambiguity of their choices could lead to an overturning of everything we know, perhaps even Father's Plan—"

"Stop."

Lucifer hadn't raised his voice, hadn't changed his tone. Faster than light, he was in front of the fledgling, danger *practically radiating off of him.*

"Look at me." Uriel raised his eyes, most likely through pure habit of following orders than any strength of will. "Humans are Father's most beloved, most inspired creation, and you think that they are flawed?"

"Not flawed!" Uriel said, panicked. "But their volatile nature makes them uncontrollable—"

"They are not supposed *to be* controlled*!" Lucifer hissed, Luce narrowing his eyes indignantly and nodding in sharp agreement. "Father intended for them to forge their own futures, to have power over their own lives." The air shimmered, six gigantic black wings manifesting behind him. Luce gaped.*

"Cool," he breathed, momentarily sidetracked.

"Lucifer—" Uriel gasped.

There was a scraping noise, like whetstones on a thousand blades. Silver spread across the edge of each feather, frosting each lethal wing. They arched higher, seemingly filling the temple with shadow and light all at once. Uriel stumbled back from the imposing image, eyes wide in terror.

"Get out." Lucifer's voice had returned to its neutral, dispassionate tone, but was barely masking the ineffable fury that trembled in every line of his body. "And you had best hope I don't inform Michael of what we spoke of here."

Uriel fled. Lucifer stretched his wings out to their fullest extent, the tips brushing the sides of the temple, before launching himself into the air. Ceilings were evidently no obstacle for angels, as Lucifer phased right through. Luce tried to follow, but something held him back as the temple began to dissolve around him...

Fragments of his dreams flashed around him, slowly coalescing into a burned wasteland that was barely recognizable as Heaven. A body crashed to the ground in front of him, wings torn and on fire. *Luce tripped away, pulse thundering in terror.*

Two figures near the edge of the battlefield caught his eye, and as Luce got closer, they sharpened into himself and...Michael?

Ro would be pleased. She always liked being right.

Gabriel and Raphael were gathering off to the side, and Luce stopped a little ways away. Too far to hear what the angels were saying, Luce nonetheless knew exactly what was happening. Voices in his memory were overlapping with the scene in front of him, tightening his throat. Luce looked away, unable to watch the pain crushing his brothers. He didn't understand how he could have been so stupid—

The sky split apart the second Michael opened the Veil. Grace washed over Luce, warm and benevolent and home. *Heaven began dissolving again, though not from the darkness that came with unconsciousness but the bright white light that came with—*

Lucifer bolted upright on the floor, eyes wide and breathing hard. Ro lifted her head slightly and then let it thump back against the wall she was slumped against.

"Oh good, you're alive," she mumbled. "Everything in working order?"

"Ro," he wheezed. "You were right."

"'Course I was." Pause. "Right about what?"

He stood slowly, Ro frowning and cracking open an eyelid. "What are you doing? You should rest."

"Don't need to," Luce said confidently. He concentrated on the image of wings he had seen in Eden, the black behemoths that spread so naturally from his back.

Nothing happened.

"What are you doing?" Ro frowned at him.

"Looking like a fool, apparently," Luce snapped, hurt. He really thought it would work…

"You are a moron," Ro mumbled. She was already falling back asleep, and Luce felt guilty for a moment. But he was having an existential crisis here!

"Ro—"

"The spell was to restore your memories, not whatever powers that might come with that," she sighed. Using the wall as support, Ro stood and took a few steps before collapsing face first onto the couch. "Go get some sleep. We can talk in the morning."

Luce sat back down on the ground, noticing the burned remains of the herbs had somehow migrated. Every chalk line was now covered in the ashes of plants, the air pungent with the smell of it. He wrinkled his nose and grabbed a blanket from the nearby chair, curling up in the centre of the pentagram. Now that the excitement and adrenaline had worn off, Luce was ready to sleep for a week.

Ro must have used a lot of energy, Luce thought as he lay facing her. The guilt returned tenfold, and he briefly recalled the amount of power he had seen swirling in her eyes. In the moment before his memories started, he could have sworn he saw a flash of white expanding from the middle of each pupil to cover the irises, like a mini supernova.

Not that it would have been a surprise. He knew Ro was powerful, and this was only more proof that she was special. Still, she didn't have to carry the burden alone, especially now that he had his memories back. Surely there must be some sort of spell, lost to humans, which could be used against Heaven? With any luck, Uriel and his followers didn't know that he remembered everything, and the two of them could use that to their advantage.

Several hundred miles away, on a quest to find their missing family, two other boys gasped awake in their hotel room. Michael and Raphael looked at each other.

"We have to go back," Rafe said simply, jumping to pack as Mike agreed grimly.

In his room, Gabriel froze where he had been writing down his latest dream as memories came crashing down on him. The disorganized journal slotted together in his mind, and he began writing again with a vengeance. If he really was the Messenger of God, he was going to do his job and deliver the damn message.

Chapter Eleven

Several hours after their memories had returned, Michael's Vauxhall Astra swung into the Elohim's driveway, screeching to a halt. Michael had barely pulled the keys from the ignition before Gabriel was barrelling out of the house. The two eldest brothers leapt out of the car in time to catch Gabe when he threw himself at them.

"Did you remember?" Gabriel demanded, refusing to let go of either of them. Michael chuckled tiredly at his impatience.

"Yes, we did. Where is Lucifer?"

Gabe went still in their arms, pulling away slowly and looking up at them searchingly. "You didn't find him? He and Ro can't have gone *that* far."

"It has been three months, brother," Raphael rumbled softly. "They know how to go to ground, and if Ro has her powers and Lucifer his memories, they will take care of themselves."

"Yeah, I know that," Gabe said, waving a hand. "The point is, they shouldn't have to."

"No, they shouldn't," Mike reassured him. "Which is why we came back to see if you have any solid leads instead of us searching aimlessly across the country. Don't get me wrong, it's satisfying to extend the road trip, but chasing Raphael through four different versions of 'Britain's Top Ten Mazes' gets a little dull after a while."

Rafe rolled his eyes at his older brother's attempt at lightening the situation, just as Carmen charged around the street corner.

"WHERE HAVE YOU BEEN AND WHERE THE HELL IS MY BEST FRIEND?"

"Thanks, Carmel," Gabe drawled.

She flapped a hand at him impatiently. "*Well*?"

"Carmen, we haven't found them yet," he held up a hand to forestall the protests, "but we thought you might have an idea as to which direction we can go."

Carmen shook her head, deflating. "Not a clue. Still, if we can't find them, then that means it's harder for others to as well, right?" No one had to ask which 'others' she meant.

The brothers glanced at each other, knowing full well that the forces of Heaven far outmatched any human means they were using to try and locate their family.

"Great," Carmen said flatly, catching the exchange. "So now what?"

"Pray?" Gabriel offered sarcastically.

Carmen stared at him delightedly. "Gabriel Elohim, I could kiss you."

"What?" he startled. "Why?"

"*Praying*. Hopefully to the one being who can put a stop to all this nonsense." She spun on her heel and darted into the Fitzgerald house, years of play dates granting her a key.

"Angels want to kill us and start the Apocalypse, Ro and Luce are in the wind, we are apparently archangels turned human, an atheist just decided to pray, and Carmel calls it nonsense." Gabriel shook his head in disbelief, grin spreading across his face. "I love that girl."

"We know," Mike and Rafe chorused.

"Everyone's known for years, Gabe, except you two," Rafe informed him gleefully.

"It was like watching Ro and Luce in a mirror," Mike added.

"Piss off," Gabe tossed over his shoulder, following Carmen. Raphael rolled his eyes and did the same, squeezing his older brother's shoulder as he went. Michael lifted his gaze to the sky.

"I hope you know what you are doing," he murmured, turning to go after the rest of his broken family.

☆

Luce woke up with a dry throat and head splitting in half. Ro snorted and fell off of the couch. He pulled the blanket over his head again.

"Ow," she groaned.

"Piss off," Luce grumbled. "You didn't have your mind expanded by aeons. You don't get to complain."

"Someone's in a bad mood," Ro muttered, getting up and stretching stiffly. "You want breakfast, or are you going to get that yourself?"

His stomach answered. "I hate you."

"No, you don't," she said easily. "Come on, I think I got us cereal as well yesterday."

"You went grocery shopping when Uriel wants us dead?"

Luce suddenly had Ro's entire attention fixed on him. "You *know* him?"

"Um," Luce stalled, shifting uncomfortably. "Maybe? I know who he is, but I'm not sure if he knows who I am, really."

"That made no sense," Ro replied. "What do you mean, he doesn't know who you are?"

"As in, he might not realize it," Luce snapped. "He shouldn't be anywhere near me or my family, but he's clearly lost all respect for us."

"Isn't Uriel an archangel?" Ro frowned. He surged to his feet, brushing aside the vertigo.

"No," he growled. "Uriel was never an archangel, never supposed to be one. If he is now, it's stolen power, nothing more."

"How do you steal power like that?" Ro rubbed her eyes. "I mean, it's sort of like ethnicity, right? Black, white, Native American, Asian, Hispanic; that kind of thing."

"It is...possible to be promoted," Luce said slowly. "But it's never happened before, and only Father has that kind of power—"

"Father?"

"God." He watched Ro pale. "What?"

"So...you are actually Lucifer? And your brothers are the other archangels? How?"

"I think...I think our Father put us here. When I was going through my memories, it looked like He interfered at the last minute. Whatever happened in Heaven, the corruption had spread far enough that we were in danger." Luce looked up at Ro. "When you were in town, did you see a payphone?"

"You have got to be joking." Ro crossed her arms. "You want to go into town and call someone? That's like sending out a beacon to every supernatural creature in the universe."

Luce raised an eyebrow. "Every creature?"

She scowled. "Enough, and they aren't exactly harmless, Luce. You shouldn't put yourself at risk like that."

"What about grocery shopping?" Luce demanded. "That wasn't risky?"

"The supernatural is far more sensitive to electromagnetic radiation than humans. Telephones, radios, infrared, even higher frequencies of radiation—they're all just tools able to track prey. It's all you are to them, Luce—easy prey." Ro shook her head, turning away.

Luce felt the knot tighten in his chest, anger forcing his body through hot and cold flashes. "So, what, it's safe for you to go out, but I am helpless and vulnerable?"

"Luce—" she sighed.

"Don't," he cut her off. "Just don't, Ro. I may not have magic powers or be an angel anymore, but that doesn't mean I'm stupid." He headed for his room. "I'm not feeling so hungry anymore. You could probably get some research done in the library."

He didn't slam the door, mostly because they were heavy metal monstrosities that took both of them or Ro's power to move. The sentiment was still there, though.

Ro avoided him for the rest of the morning.

Ro slammed the next book shut with none of her usual care for ancient texts. With all of her newfound power, she should be able to do something useful.

In the centre of the table, the plainest—and possibly the most modern—volume in the bunker lay innocently. Ro eyed it warily, and then gave in. She dragged the Bible forward, begrudgingly opening to somewhere in the middle. Having no idea what she was looking for, Ro was hoping it would mention a problem similar to theirs.

A couple hours later, she was ready to throw the unhelpful, religiously smug book into the river. All it had done was ramble on about moral lessons and the creation of things and floods and a piece about Lucifer's fall she had skipped over.

In hindsight, it might have something important, but she really didn't want to read a misinterpretation with the actual (albeit former) angel four floors above her. She sighed and slowly flipped the pages, head barely held up by her hand.

"Revelation," she murmured. Wasn't that the bit about the Apocalypse? She leaned forward, slightly more awake than she felt five minutes ago.

Hell, Heaven, destruction of Earth…nothing concrete. This was why she didn't like monotheistic religions, and some polytheistic ones. The people in charge liked to ramble about random and inane topics, like the weather, instead of being educational and halfway helpful.

Although, it did raise an interesting question: if the Apocalypse was supposed to be a war between the Powers of Heaven and Hell, why were the angels coming after humans? And where were all the demons?

Not that she wanted demons around; Ro would be happy if they stayed in Hell for all eternity. Except demons didn't do that, regardless of how scared they were of Wiccans.

Maybe they aren't as scared of Wiccans as much as they are of angels.

Which…was kind of terrifying. If angels worried demons enough that they kept their heads down, then what chance did Ro and Luce have against Heaven? Maybe they weren't even topside. Typical demons, cowering in hellfire while the angels razed the rest of the planet.

Ro had no illusions about getting the demons to help them. Even if she thought working with demons was a good idea, Earth would most likely be destroyed. And then Hell's army would turn on whatever was left of humanity.

Assuming they won. If she had to guess, the only reason the angels weren't storming Hell was because they were hunting Ro and Luce. If she could redirect their attention…

Ro looked around the library. Surely, in subjects this extensive, there had to be records of Hell and demons, right? While she really didn't want to consider why or how her father had gotten all of these things (assuming it had been her father. If the military had collected these, she would be forced to investigate what the hell—no pun intended—the government thought it was doing), it was immensely helpful and she would want to move in if it wasn't in the outback of British civilization.

Hell would be near the back, if the pattern held steady. Ro had no clue if there was a system, but hopefully Hell would be included and not hidden away in a separate room like the military's dirty little secret.

Okay, so she might be overreacting. Slightly.

Thankfully, there was a section, although it wasn't very big. It made up for the lack of size in age. Some of them were written in hieroglyphics, and must have been translated from cuneiform tablets because one or two symbols were definitely not traditional Egyptian. Now she just needed to find a multilingual dictionary...

Luce glanced at his watch, grateful that it was still working after being nearly crushed by stone. Ro had been holed up in the library for almost the entire morning, which meant that she wasn't coming up for air. Unless something was really interesting, she tended to break from research anywhere from three to four hours at a time. Five hours in and there was nothing that could pull her away.

Of course, Carmen and the Elohims always tried, and Luce was usually able to persuade her that sleeping and eating was a good thing, but this time Ro's obsessive behaviour actually worked in his favour.

When he had gone hunting, Luce wore all the clothes Ro had given him. Today, he wore the only normal, modern clothes he could find in the bunker; a tee, jeans, trainers, and a jumper. His only concession was the cloak, but he wasn't about to go out looking like a time travelling drunkard.

He quietly headed for the door, pausing by the stairway to see if Ro was coming back up. Hearing nothing, Luce opened the door as carefully as humanly (he mentally sneered at the word before immediately feeling like a horrible person. Angel. Whatever) possible, slipping out between only a few centimetres of space and shutting it just as carefully.

The road into town was a few miles outside the pseudo barrier. The car was parked in the 'driveway' that stopped metres from the actual bunker. Luce belatedly checked his pockets, breathing a sigh of relief when he found the keys. Unfortunately, any change that might have accumulated had vanished somewhere between his house and the Thames. It may have been spent on petrol, he couldn't remember.

He would have to ask one of the shopkeepers to use their phone. With any luck, Luce would be back at the bunker in twenty minutes and Ro would never know he was gone. She worried about him far too much; he was perfectly capable of taking care of himself.

Downstairs, Ro let out a shaky breath and leaned back in her chair. Eyes scratchy from the dim lighting, she nevertheless couldn't stop smiling. If this worked, if she could pull this off…they could go home. She and Luce could stop running and go back to school and be mostly normal. They could stop looking over their shoulders all the time. They could see their *family*.

She made it sound like they had been gone for years. Sometimes it felt like that.

The spell wasn't overly complicated, physically. All she would need was her blood smeared on an inverted pentagram drawn in chalk and a chant in Latin, which she could translate back from the inconveniently modern English version in the book. It was the metaphysical part that Ro would have trouble with.

All hell magicks went against every Wiccan teaching in existence, and opening the gates to hell and sending beings in—even corrupted ones—would leave a deep taint on her soul. A lot of anger, a lot of hate, was required to fuel a spell this dark.

If Ro thought of her grandmother, she was pretty sure she could conjure up sufficient emotional distress.

Even so…using evil magicks so soon after manifesting was dangerous—witch dangerous. Those that had turned to dark magicks became cut off from the natural earth; losing the connection that had given them power and replacing it with a contaminated one, an infection spreading that eventually consumed their very mind.

It didn't matter. If necessary, she would sacrifice herself in an instant. If it would save Luce, she would sacrifice anything.

He just couldn't know about it.

Luce stepped into the back room of the supermarket; the only shop with a phone available for public use in this tiny town. He couldn't stop twitching, forcing him to redial twice. Eventually it rang, and Luce could barely breathe as someone picked up the phone.

"Hello?" The achingly familiar voice was irritated, in a way only their family and their girls were able to tell. Michael often tried to cover up his annoyance with politeness, although it was Lucifer who could get rid of people quickly by making them as uncomfortable as possible. His eldest brother had weird hang-ups about hurting people's feelings.

Lucifer swallowed heavily, throat clicking as his eyes tightened. The phone slipped in his sweaty grip. Michael quickly lost patience, uncharacteristically.

"Look, if you don't mind, I really don't have time for—"

"*Michael*," Lucifer whispered.

Dead silence. Then.

"WHERE THE HELL HAVE YOU BEEN? DO YOU KNOW HOW WORRIED WE ARE? SO HELP YOU FATHER, LUCIFER—"

"Michael, it's Uriel," he said brokenly. "Uriel and Raziel and the whole damn *Host*, they want us dead and I don't understand—"

"Where are you?" Michael asked, tone gentling. Lucifer let out a half sob.

"Don't. We're doing everything we can from here, but it's too dangerous right now." It was killing him, not having his brothers here, but as long as Heaven was focused on him and Ro, his family was relatively safe.

"Carmen thinks she might have something. We'll check it out, but then we're coming to find you, Lucifer," Michael promised. Lucifer smiled weakly, even though Mike couldn't see it.

"I know. May the wind be steady beneath your wings."

"May your sword sharpen on the bone of your enemies," Michael returned grimly.

Luce breathed thickly through his nose and hung up. He had to get back to the bunker.

He didn't even make it to the car.

Ro frowned and looked up at the ceiling. It sounded like someone was…knocking? Who would even know the bunker existed, let alone where it was or that someone was in here? She jogged up the stairs, grabbing the dagger from her room as she passed it. Opening the door and tensing for a fight, it took a second for Ro to realize exactly who was in front of her.

"Oh stars, *Luce*," she gasped, tugging him and the person who brought him back inside.

"He said this was where he was staying just before he passed out," the woman said quietly. Ro glanced up at her and turned her attention back to her friend. Clearly, the woman didn't think this was a fit place for children to stay on their own.

Screw her.

"Yeah, he is. We are. Thank you for bringing him back safely," Ro smiled falsely, just wanting to get rid of the local.

"No problem." She stuck her hands in her pockets; obviously, she wasn't planning on going anywhere. "I'm Ariel, by the way."

"Great," Ro said, patience fading. "If you don't mind, I'm going to take care of my friend now."

Ariel nodded easily. "Some bloke attacked him. Albino, about yea high; ring any bells?"

"Too many," Ro scowled. "Is he gone?"

"Yup; Chief Constable Bill scared him off with his shotgun."

Ro doubted that. Angels didn't exactly have anything to fear from shotguns. "Did anyone follow you? How many people know we're here?"

"Relax, kid. No one followed me, and even though the town noticed new folks, not many people know about the military bunker.

Even fewer know where it is. The Chief Constable and his Deputy are about it." She smiled, evidently trying to be reassuring.

It wasn't working. "Then how do you know—" Ro stopped, taking Ariel in fully for the first time since she walked in the door. The Wiccan had no clue how she missed the black uniform or the *gun holster*, but the badge pinned to Ariel's lapel cleared any doubts Ro might have had about her vocation.

"Oh." They were so screwed.

"Where are your parents?" Ariel wasn't pulling her punches anymore, and if Ro wasn't careful, this would get them all killed.

"Look, I don't—"

Ro was interrupted by Luce groaning and stirring, still slumped in her arms. She briefly glanced at the Deputy Chief, and then proceeded to ignore her in favour of settling Luce on the couch.

"As much as I appreciate the concern, Constable, I have to take care of my friend. So if you don't mind..."

"But I do mind. A couple of kids shouldn't be all on their own up here, and it's private property anyway—"

"It's my dad's," Ro blurted. Ariel paused and raised a sceptical eyebrow. "And yes, it is private property, and you really need to leave now. Feel free to come back at a later date."

"Kid—" Ariel tried.

"Look, I really don't have time for this. If you need a statement or something, then I will get it to you. However, at the moment my hands are full, and I am perfectly capable of protecting myself and my friend," Ro snapped, turning her attention back to Luce.

Ariel's eyes narrowed. "Protect against what?"

Ro's patience finally snapped, and she turned cold eyes on the Deputy. "You need to leave. Trust me; you don't want to get caught up in this. If I were you, I'd get as far away from this bunker as possible. But if you don't walk out that door in the next seven seconds, I will forcefully remove you from my property. Understand?"

Ariel stiffened and eyed the Wiccan coolly. "Threatening a policewoman isn't very smart, Miss...?"

"Leave. I won't ask again." Ro glared at Ariel. The Deputy's mouth quirked sadly as she held her hands up in supplication.

"You aren't on your own, kid. Whatever the two of you are running from, the Corris police department can help," Ariel said softly.

"I doubt that," Ro said, dismissing the other woman.

"You might be surprised," Ariel tossed over her shoulder. Ro frowned and locked the door behind her. She fetched her pouch from the trunk in her room, grabbing the first aid kit as an afterthought. Until she could figure out what had happened to him, however, Ro wasn't going to use any medication or potion on Luce.

As if she didn't already have enough incentive. Those angelic bastards were going to Hell; for good, if Ro could manage it.

Luce drifted. Occasionally, he'd catch someone murmuring to him, coaxing him awake for a few minutes, forcing liquids down his throat. For the most part, he felt like a mind without a body, except when something pressed down on it and he flared in pain.

He slept.

Her friend was finally resting, and Ro had done all she could for Luce's injuries. She slipped out of the bedroom, wondering why a military bunker would not have an infirmary. Did the architects just assume no one was going to get hurt, or that they'd miraculously heal?

Of course, it was supposed to be a fallout bunker adapted for research purposes, but what kind of excuse was that? Maybe there had been an infirmary, and when the troops came to redecorate, they put the library there instead or something.

Ro knew this line of thought wasn't relevant, but she was trying to distract herself from Luce's condition and what she was about to do. Obviously, it wasn't working very well.

In the secondary library—on the main floor, not the big one—she had the spell book, the translation, and the supplies she had gathered. Ro had to go outside for this spell, which was probably for the best. Regardless of what the spell intended, she was opening a gate to Hell.

And she didn't really want angels being sucked into the bunker. Especially when they were pissed and in close quarters with Luce and herself.

The ravine where she had found Luce hunting before would work. It was right near the border and with only one way out besides flying. Ro breathed in deeply before gathering up the black dress from her grandmother's attic. She hadn't had occasion to wear it, but seeing as it was a ceremonial outfit that made sense.

She didn't want to wear it at all, but changed quickly nonetheless. Hopefully it would offer some measure of protection during the ritual. The two books—the one from the bunker and her Grimoire—she stuffed in the pack along with the spell box. For the most part, it only contained healing herbs and potions, but there were some poisons like belladonna and hemlock and monkshood. Ro didn't know the specifics of angel biology, but hopefully this would slow them down at least enough for her to open the portal.

Ro peeked in on Luce one more time before heading out, smiling softly at the adorable picture. For as long as she could remember, when Luce had slept deeply, he always sprawled across whatever surface he had collapsed on and buried his face in the nearest soft object. Occasionally he'd let out a quiet snuffling noise and melt even further. Seriously, it looked like all the bones had disappeared from his body.

This was why she had to perform the spell. For Luce, and more chances to rest without worry or fear or the possibility of being attacked at any moment. Ro shut off the light and closed the bedroom door. With any luck, this wouldn't take too long and everything could go back to normal. Or semi-normal anyway; normal for a Wiccan and four Judeo-Christian archangels.

Ro tossed the cloak around her shoulders and hefted the bag. Once she committed to the spell she couldn't change her mind. She sighed and allowed herself to slump for a few seconds before straightening and walking out of the bunker.

Heaven was going to regret screwing with Rowan Fitzgerald.

Chapter Twelve

Luce stirred, waking fully for the first time in several days. He frowned into the darkness.

"Ro?" Nothing. Either she had left to do something elsewhere in the bunker or she was finally sleeping instead of taking care of him. The horrible feeling knotting his intestines gave Luce the idea that something was wrong with Ro.

Or he could just be feeling sick again. Unfortunately, nothing was that easy for them these days.

Which meant Ro was most likely in trouble.

"Damn it," Luce muttered, immediately wincing. Should he swear if he used to be an archangel? Was he technically still one? Would God smite him for cursing? Okay, if God was going to smite him, it probably would have been during the whole rebellion debacle, but still.

Luce was getting distracted. He needed to find Ro.

He staggered to his feet, still weak from the injuries Uriel had given him. When he got his Splendour back, he was so kicking the seraph into next century. Luce slowly made his way through the bunker, frown increasing with every empty room. If Ro wasn't here…

Shit.

☆

Ro peered up at the clouds, tasting the heaviness of oncoming rain. She checked the translation one last time, muttering the English out loud: "Ancient powers, I call upon you: open the gate to hell. I command you to deliver those who forsake God to eternal perdition."

She dragged the small dagger along her forearm, wincing at the fiery threads of pain she hadn't bothered to dull with extra magic. She watched her blood drip to the ground with vague interest; right now, a little blood seemed like a small price to pay in order to get what she wanted. Black sparks swirled into the air when the liquid hit the lines burned into the rock. The grass had withered and the dirt had blown away as soon as she completed the pentagram, tainted and fleeing the evil about to arrive.

This had better work.

"*Antiqua munia, obsecro vos: porta inferni aperta. Iubeō te ut liberare et qui dereliquerunt Dominum aeternae perditionis.*" Ro's voice shook as the wind began to pick up, the trees thrashing wildly above her. She glanced up fearfully, swallowing heavily before clearing her throat.

"*Antiqua munia, obsecro vos: porta inferni aperta. Iubeō te ut liberare et qui dereliquerunt Dominum aeternae perditionis!*" Ro's confidence grew slightly, although she was still shaking. Though that might be because she was still bleeding.

Squeezing her eyes shut and therefore not seeing the figure at the top of the ravine, Ro steeled herself for the last repetition.

Antiqua munia, obsecro vos: porta inferni aperta!

Iubeō te ut liberare et qui dereliquerunt Dominum aeternae perditionis!

The bedrock cracked open, throwing Ro back into the wall. Hellfire licked at the edges of the chasm, screams echoing around the forest. Smoke billowed into the sky, indistinguishable forms writhing within. Ro held her breath, horrified, and then—

The shadows exploded, whips of darkness lashing out into the world. The abyss groaned as it sealed, and the grove returned to its previous state. Ro didn't move.

Luce climbed down, loose pebbles announcing his presence. She didn't look at him, still staring at the burnt and bloody ground. He said nothing, just wrapped an arm around her shivering body. Every second that passed etched haunted lines into Ro's features, and Luce could do nothing to stop it.

"That wasn't supposed to happen," Ro eventually protested. Her voice was scratchy from power, her eyes still dark with terror. "The spell was supposed to trap the disobedient angels in Hell, not release damnation on the earth."

Luce struggled to keep his silence, understanding that his friend didn't need words at the moment.

"I must have...done something wrong, picked the wrong spell—"

"*Ut liberare*," Luce said quietly, unable to hold his peace. Ro twisted to look at him.

"What?" she frowned.

"Ut liberare. *To liberate*, not deliver. To deliver is *ut liberaret*." Luce shook his head roughly. "You should have told me, Ro; that's what I'm here for. To help you, to support you, to hold you up and hold you back when I need to. Why didn't you trust me?"

"I do trust you!" she protested immediately, vehemently. "I wasn't even sure it would work, and then you got hurt—"

"So you decided you were going to throw the gates of Hell wide open?" Luce was trying so hard to stay calm, to not punish Ro because he knew she was already punishing herself enough. But they had too many problems to deal with already.

"I had no idea that was going to happen!" Ro drew away from him in shock. Luce's mouth tightened.

"You should have double checked your work! Did you even pay attention to the original translation, or did you do half and decide that was good enough?" What the hell was he doing, this was only going to make things worse, but he was so *angry*—

"Screw you, Lucifer!" Ro shot to her feet, Luce following shortly after. "How dare you accuse me of not trying! For *months* I have been trying to find a solution, on top of helping you with your memories and trying to keep us, if not healthy, then at least *alive*! Don't ever presume that I don't care. I may be desperate, and I made a mistake, but you aren't exactly perfect either!"

He took a step back in shock. "What is that supposed to mean?"

Ro advanced on him, matching him stride for stride until the boy was pressed against the ravine wall. “It means that everything I did, I did for my family, the people I love, and you have done no less to protect your own. Hell, you started a feud that ripped Heaven apart because you were standing up for what was right. My actions are no different.”

“Stop it,” Luce growled, full-blown wrath stirring in his chest now. Ro glared at him for a long moment, then stormed back to the bunker in disgust. Luce let out a shaky breath and sagged against the rock, closing his eyes against the burning wetness on his face.

At this rate, things were never going to be alright again.

“Luce?” Ro ventured, knowing that while they were still upset with each other, the two of them had never cut the other out of their life completely; not about something important. Maybe. She hoped.

“Yes, Ro?” Lucifer’s tone was cool, and while Ro deserved it, it still made her wince.

“I was wondering…would you tell me about Heaven? About what it was like when you were archangels, and you were happy together?” Ro’s voice was shy, and Luce softened a little in response.

“Sure,” he said, scooting aside to make room for the young Wiccan. She sat gingerly, still cautious around him. It hurt that they had come to this, so untrusting when they had once depended on the other without reservation or hesitation. “Heaven was…Heaven. Beautiful, peaceful—but never boring, we learned quickly after the first souls arrived to never let them get bored—and humans could carve out their own little corner and mould it to their desires; create their own private worlds to spend eternal bliss in.” Luce sighed. “It is difficult to explain in any human language the splendour and atmosphere of Heaven. Most of it has to be experienced. Now, what do you want to know, specifically?”

“Do you sit on clouds and play harps?” she asked seriously—except for the glint in her eye. He scowled in mock offence.

“Gabriel does,” he replied slyly. “But no, for the most part we are warriors of the Lord; Heaven’s greatest weapons. Our power is greater than any angel of the two lower classes, and that's usually represented by our wings."

"Three pairs, right?"

Luce nodded. "The first is what we usually show to everyone, regardless of status or function or circumstance. The second most commonly appears when we are fighting, as they help us in battle. In extreme conditions—severe wars and times of great emotional distress—the third pair appears."

"How do wings help you in battle?" Ro asked sceptically. "Do you whack them in the face and blind them with feathers?"

Luce snorted. "Closer than you think. The edges of our feathers hone to edges roughly the thickness of a quark—it's the way we hide ourselves from sight, by cutting through the visible wavelengths of electromagnetic radiation—and the more pairs you have, the greater your strength when it comes to splitting the matter of the universe. And time, in the archangels' case."

"You can *time travel*?" Ro screeched. Luce flinched back and rubbed his ears, glaring at Ro reprovingly. She glared back indignantly, completely unabashed.

"Extreme cases. It takes all three wings, and a hell of a lot more power than we would be willing to spend on casual trips through the time continuum. Besides, there are rules even *we* have to follow, and changing time isn't allowed. Nor is allowing you to know your own future."

"If knowing the future is forbidden, why do prophecies exist?" Ro tilted her head to the side in confusion, much like a small bird.

"Don't ask me; Gabriel's the bloody Messenger of the Lord. He's in charge of prophecies and proclamations and all that stuff." Luce shrugged.

"Okay. If you aren't allowed to do anything, why do you have the ability to travel in time in the first place?" Ro folded her arms triumphantly, raising an eyebrow in defiance.

"We use it mostly to watch important moments in human history, if we need to double check something or forgot crucial information, and to teach younger angels. They understand it better if they aren't forced to read from a dusty book," Luce grimaced in sympathy.

Ro stared at him blankly. "So, basically, you're using it like a really time consuming, battery wasting 3D television documentary?

Haven't you heard of the rewind feature? Why the hell hasn't Heaven invested in DVR yet?"

"You're missing the point, Ro," Luce sighed. She rolled her eyes.

"Fine. So Heaven doesn't like modern technology; noted. Does that mean you lot still use swords?"

"As far as I'm aware," Luce said. "All angels carried a blade—a simple dagger that worked against any beings of equal or lesser power—and had the ability to summon a Sword crafted from their own Splendour that would protect them to the best of its ability. They had...impressions of their wielder's consciousness, so they were almost sentient and never worked for another being, unless the wielder approved of the use."

"So you haven't graduated to Flaming Pistols or anything. And you have the nerve to call humans primitive? At least we use our ingenuity to come up with more creative ways to kill each other off." Ro rolled her eyes and flopped back with a huff.

"Always a good thing," Luce replied dryly. His shoulders stiffened and icy eyes cooled even further with his next remark. "No wonder so many of you become demons later."

Ro's eyes flashed, and Luce had no time to prepare himself before her fist connected with his nose. Blood spurted as Ro stormed out of the room, ignoring Lucifer's pained curses.

She sighed. The tension was mounting exponentially between them. They hadn't fought this badly since...forever. The last time anything like this kind of strain coloured their interactions was the brief period halfway through sixth year. She hated it.

Ro wondered exactly what day it was, or even the month. Had their families still celebrated their winter holidays? Michael and Raphael would most definitely be home by now, and the adults would likely be terrorizing (or manipulating, in Kali's case) the Ministry of Defense into mobilizing. Carmen and Gabriel would have applied to universities and maybe even gotten accepted. She hoped they would go to schools near each other, if not the same university. They deserved happiness.

She and Luce...they would never go back to the way things were before. Too much had changed, *they* had changed, and the thought of finishing secondary school made Ro laugh bitterly. Even going to university...

They were too much like warriors now, though if Ro suggested joining the military Luce might literally bite her head off. Neither of them were very good at following orders.

And Luce didn't belong down here, among the mortals. He belonged in the stars, light and grace and love and ice. Humans were messy and ephemeral and cruel, and he had been tossed down to join them unjustly.

Ro stepped into the library for the first time since the ritual, determined to find a way to restore Lucifer's Splendour. He deserved it.

Chapter Thirteen

Carmen could barely sit still through the last class of the day. Only two weeks until Senior Preliminary Exams, and Luce and Ro were still missing. Michael and Raphael had returned yesterday from chasing yet another false lead, and Gabriel was growing ever more despondent. The uncertain fate of his twin was really taking its toll on him.

The bell finally rang, and Carmen practically sprinted to her locker. The Fitzgeralds and the Elohims were both spending all their time and energy on finding the two missing teens, but despite months of searching and endless nights of praying, they had nothing to show for it. And despite her amazing hacking skills, even Carmen was having trouble finding a God who, for all intents and purposes, was effectively human and probably didn't know any differently.

She slammed the locker door, eager to get home and do more research. Carmen spun towards the doors—

And nearly ran into someone. Craning her neck back, Carmen groaned internally before pasting on a clearly fake smile. Well, fake for anyone with eyes to see, which apparently didn't apply to one Vincent Bassano.

"Can I help you?" She really did need to get home. Vincent, it seemed, did not agree with that sentiment.

"You're in my English class," he said bluntly. She waited. When he didn't elaborate, Carmen raised an eyebrow.

"Yes, and?"

Vincent shuffled nervously in front of her. "I was wondering if you could help me with the paper we're doing..." He trailed off, glancing up at her hopefully through his eyelashes. When she met his gaze, he quickly looked back down at his shoes, scuffing the tile.

"Sorry," Carmen said briskly. "I've got a lot going on right now; I barely get my own homework done as it is. Ask Jody Locke; she tutors other kids, so she'll be able to help you." Somehow, Carmen didn't really care about school anymore, and she really didn't have the energy to make someone else care.

She jogged out into the car-park, dodging cars to meet Gabe at his. Her heart panged as she remembered a time when the biggest worry any of them had was who had slashed Gabriel's tires. Now, everyone was frantic over Ro and Luce, and Carmen was at the end of her rope.

It didn't help that the Elohims were hiding something. The brothers weren't obvious about it, of course, but Carmen had grown up with them. She knew when they weren't telling her something. The more important the secret was, the worse they were at keeping it.

She would have a chance to crack them later, but for the moment Carmen needed to focus on her best friend. Willow was attempting another scrying session this afternoon, and she wasn't going to miss it. Especially not for tutoring.

"It's hopeless," Willow sighed, getting a glass of water from her kitchen. Maps of the world were pasted on every wall, a pendant Ro had gotten for her fifteenth birthday lying innocently on the table in the centre of the room. The older woman leaned back against the counter wearily, sweat dripping from the ends of her hair.

"Maybe we should try a different focus?" Carmen suggested, inexplicably guilty.

Willow shook her head. "No, that's not the problem. The spell, the focus, isn't the weak spot in this. I'm running into a wall every time I try to cast. Someone's blocking me, and I have to believe it's my idiot niece. The good news is that she isn't dead."

"How do you know?" Carmen asked, instantly regretting saying anything.

"I've searched for dead people before; that's not what this feels like," Willow sighed. "Something's definitely there; think of it like a stone wall instead of just a void."

"Okay," Carmen said slowly. "Well, we know they haven't left the country, at least by any obvious means. No tickets for boat or plane, no cameras caught them at major checkpoints; if they crossed borders, it wasn't legally. Or mundanely." She frowned. "Is that a word?"

"Perhaps we are relying too much on the mundane," Willow suggested, staring at the maps. "If Ro had to flee her home, and knew something powerful was chasing her, and she was scared—"

"And had someone else to look after," Carmen cut in. "We should think like Ro, instead of assuming hypothetical situations. Okay," Carmen stared at the maps. "If I were Ro, fleeing for my life with my boyfriend, where would I go to feel safe?"

Michael closed the door to his room behind him, turning to face his brothers. Gabriel had sprawled over the bed while Raphael perched at Michael's desk. The eldest brother crossed the room to lean against the window. He stared down at the street, wishing that Lucifer and Ro would come up the pavement, laughing like they always did.

Of course, that didn't happen. Michael sighed and tuned into the conversation behind him.

"—what else we *can* do!" Raphael and Gabriel squared off, the younger glaring fiercely at his brother. Michael sighed again, feeling his composure rapidly slipping away.

"We don't give up, that's for sure!" Gabriel's face was drawn, far older than it had any right to be. "As long as they aren't here, with their family, we should be working to bring them home. Especially if they're in danger."

Raphael scowled, but Michael interrupted before the argument could dissolve into violence and cruel words. "Enough. Gabriel is right; we should find Lucifer and Ro, and we shouldn't stop for any reason. However," he added at Gabe's triumphant look. "Raphael has a point. Almost everything we've tried, that Willow and Carmen have tried, has failed. Beyond Carmen hacking the military and giving the order to search the world over with a fine-tooth comb, I don't know what else we can do."

"So have Carmel hack the military," Gabe demanded, shrugging casually when Raphael looked at him in askance. "What? It's not like she hasn't done it before."

"I was hoping for something a little less drastic," Michael pointed out mildly.

"Like what? Finding God and bringing His wrath down on Heaven?" Raphael asked. Michael had always been impressed at his brother's ability to be sarcastic while seeming completely serious, but this was taking it to a whole new level.

"Pretty much, yeah," Carmen announced cheerfully, barging into Michael's room with the laptop in hand. "I think I found Him. Or should I say, Her."

"What?" Gabriel was the only brother with the presence of mind to voice their confusion. Possibly because he interacted with Carmen on a daily basis and therefore knew how to react.

"I figured that God wasn't actually giving these orders. Ergo, He wasn't in Heaven. So, I looked for people born roughly around the time you four were supposed to be. I cross-referenced the list with medical and psychiatric records—yes, I used government resources to get them; don't look at me like that, Raphael! It's for the greater good—as well as news broadcasts and articles. Once I narrowed it down to a few people, it was just a matter of figuring out who the most likely candidate was." Carmen settled on the bed, dislodging a disgruntled Gabriel, and put her computer in her lap.

"Which is…?" Raphael asked. Carmen looked up, startled.

"Girl in Edinburgh. Name of Evelyn Smyth. And before you ask, yes, I'm sure."

"Why her?" Michael asked, peering over Gabriel's shoulder as Raphael crowded in on her other side.

"Well, your names aren't exactly subtle. The first names are identical to your heavenly ones, and Elohim means 'of God.' I figured God wanted to leave clues in case you ever figured it out. Evelyn means 'life;' Smyth is a derivative of—"

"Smith, from families of smithing businesses," Gabriel cut in excitedly. "Literally, Life Smith. She might as well have set off a flare."

Carmen rolled her eyes. "Yeah, whatever, hotshot. I'm still the one who found Her, with good old-fashioned human ingenuity and machinery at that. You lot were so caught up in the mysticism that you forgot to look for the obvious. And so did the angels."

"They don't know?" Michael was surprised. The angels he commanded hadn't been that bad. What had happened to Heaven?

"Hang on—'your heavenly ones?'" Raphael stared at Carmen, who just looked back, amused. "What does that mean?"

"It means you're archangels of the Lord. Congrats," Carmen added belatedly. The brothers gaped at her.

"You *know*?" Gabe squeaked. Michael hadn't known his brother's voice could go that high. Maybe Carmen just had that effect on him.

"It wasn't hard. I knew you three were hiding something; you aren't that subtle, and I know you boys. From there it was just a matter of logic. And thinking like Ro."

"Why would you want to think like Ro?" Michael had to agree with Raphael on that point. Ro's mind was a scary, scary place to be.

"I was trying to figure out where she went. Instead I got her sarcastic voice in my head telling me that you are all idiotic celestial beings and you need to focus on the bigger picture. I think it was her version of an answering machine," Carmen shrugged, turning her attention back to her screen.

"Yeah, that sounds like Ro," Gabe agreed, paying more attention to Carmen. Raphael rolled his eyes as Michael hid a smile.

"So, let's go find God, and convince Her to kick some angelic arse," Carmen declared, snapping the laptop closed and hopping off the bed. She waved over her shoulder. "Bright and early tomorrow morning, people! Willow said she'd inform the parentals, so don't worry."

"Yes, because that's what we should be worried about," Raphael deadpanned.

Carmen's laughter floated up to them, cutting off as the door closed. Gabe groaned and flopped back onto the bed, an arm thrown over his face dramatically. Michael shoved him off, Raphael snorting at his little brother's flailing.

"I hate you both," Gabe grumbled, grinning.

The boy previously known as Vincent Bassano stood at the corner of Crawford and Union Street. Eyes glinting with inhuman light followed Carmen Feye as she let herself into her house. The creature didn't move, even as another form stepped up beside him.

"This girl is not our target," once-Jody Locke said, though her gaze fixed hungrily on the door. The older demon said nothing.

"We should be focused—" she tried again.

"They will lead us to them," Kokabiel stated, the demon falling silent. Most demons, made of twisted human souls, were in awe of the fallen angels. Lilith seemed to be the one exception, but then she was the eldest, and most fallen angels were alternately terrified and envious of her. Adam's first wife who had refused to bow down to man, and to God, had become a model for the rebellious angels.

"You are sure?" Eligos asked hesitantly. Despite her position as a Duke of Hell, Kokabiel was still of higher rank than she.

He stared at her. "If not to our Lord and the witch with him, then they will lead us to angels. We simply must wait for them to make the first move."

"Of course," Eligos soothed hastily. She fidgeted with the hem of her top and rolled her neck. "How much longer must we stay in these bodies? I want—"

"Be silent," Kokabiel ordered. "Until our Lord is restored to his Splendour and the armies of Heaven have been decimated, we must conceal ourselves among the humans. Although," a savage grin split his childish features, "we might as well have a little fun beforehand."

"Sir?"

"When the archangels and their pet human leave, destroy the town. Make it painful, draw it out, and let it be noticed." Kokabiel turned to the demon. "Might as well let them know the End of Days is upon them."

"Of course, sir." Eligos smiled, lips splitting to reveal bloody teeth. "Shall I loose the Hounds on them, as well?"

He waved a negligent hand, once more focused on the Feye residence. "Do what you will, after the children leave. We wouldn't want to harm them and ruin our chances of finding our Lord."

Eligos nodded, stepping back into the shadows and disappearing to another plane. Kokabiel carefully put the human shell he inhabited in stasis, freezing the organs and diverting a little of his tarnished Splendour to the muscles so they would not deteriorate as quickly. It wouldn't do for him to require a new meat suit every few weeks, especially with a war on. Not using a fraction of energy to preserve this body while he needed one, when he had plenty to spare, was a very stupid move. And Kokabiel did not consider himself stupid.

The fallen angel allowed himself a small grin and murmured softly, "Tick tock, little humans. Time to come out and play…"

"You are absolutely sure our parents are okay with this?" Gabriel asked dubiously as he heaved the duffels into the Astra's boot. Carmen huffed.

"Yes, Gabe, I'm sure. Willow convinced my parents it was fine because the three of you would be with me, and your parents were surprisingly cool with it. Can we go now?"

"Yes, we can," Raphael said, climbing into the passenger seat. "It will only take about half a day to make a round trip, Gabriel. It's not like we're going to London or anything."

"Raphael is right," Michael said, turning the ignition as Gabriel and Carmen climbed into the back seat. "They would have refused if this didn't resemble a school trip so much."

"How many God-searching school trips have you been on?" Gabriel asked incredulously.

"Not the point, Gabe," Raphael sighed. "Just please, don't turn this into the holiday of '03. Once was more than enough."

"Hey, we had fun!"

"Yes, taking fifty showers because I was covered in Cheez Whiz was the highlight of my life."

"Do you two have to start already?" Michael sighed, glancing irritably at his brothers.

"I don't think they know any other way to interact," Carmen put in helpfully. The sentiment was somewhat marred by the snickers she couldn't control.

Michael sighed again. This was going to be a long drive.

Uriel turned away from the floor-to-ceiling windows overlooking Heaven as Raziel entered his office. "What is it?"

"Sir, the other archangels are moving, as well as the human girl. Sources report that they are headed for the city of Edinburgh, in search of a crucial ally."

"What ally?" Uriel asked sharply.

"We don't know, sir," Raziel replied nervously. Being in the archangel's office always made him feel uncomfortable, as if he was about to be fired, even though he was pretty sure angels couldn't actually be fired. The office was just too...corporate. Industrial. There was no emotion, no sentiment. For beings of pure feeling, it was very unsettling. "Simply that they expressed hope that this person could help them. They were very unspecific."

"Follow them," Uriel said immediately, sitting behind his glass-topped desk. "Every detail must be observed, and if new information comes to light, inform me. If this ally proves to be dangerous, we may be forced to take action."

"Sir?" Raziel frowned.

"We can't allow for the possibility of injury coming to our esteemed leaders, can we? A threat to the archangels must be eliminated." Uriel waved a hand in dismissal. "Go. Do not return without more information."

The lower angel bowed slightly and exited. Uriel allowed himself a small smirk and swivelled around to gaze upon his domain.

"Well, well, this *will* be fun."

"You are absolutely sure this is the right house?" Gabriel asked as they stared. Carmen scowled.

"Why are you doubting me all of a sudden? Yes, I'm sure. It just…isn't what we expected." They stared some more.

The shabby brick townhouse with its peeling shutters, patchy roof shingles, and scraggly four by four plot of grass that passed for a front lawn didn't inspire awe. Indeed, it seemed more likely to house a drug addict or an alcoholic or even a sociopathic war veteran rather than the human incarnation of God. Still, the address was listed under the name of one Evelyn Smyth, so there was nothing for it.

Michael, being the eldest, was forced to make the first move when none of the others seemed about to. He hesitantly raised a fist to knock, half-certain the wood would shatter at the slightest touch. The other three looked ready to bolt at the first sign of life.

The door disappeared, replaced by a red-haired woman glowering at them underneath freckles. Even though she was the same age as them, her green eyes were still superimposed by glasses, and lines gathered at the corners. Strands of silver wove through the red, and her clothes were dirty and stained.

"Yes?" she snapped when none of them said anything. "What do you want?"

"Er…" Michael faltered.

Carmen jumped in as the woman visibly lost patience. "Are you Evelyn Smyth?"

"Maybe." The girl grew, if anything, even warier. "What's it to you?"

"We were hoping we could talk to you," Carmen said brightly, undeterred by the sharp tone. "We have a bit of a situation, and hoped you could give us some advice."

"I don't give advice," Evelyn said flatly, still not slamming the door in their faces.

"Please, just hear us out," Michael said, finally recovering his voice. Evelyn looked at them all for a long moment, frowning at the Elohims.

"Fine. Come in. I'll make some juice. When I finish my glass, your continued stay depends on how convincing you are." She spun on her heel and disappeared back into the house.

The four teens sagged in relief, quickly following before Evelyn could change her mind.

The inside of the house was as decrepit as the outside; rough floorboards dragged at their shoes, scraps of wallpaper clung to corners, exposed outlets and lamp wires sparked as they passed. Carmen shifted closer to Gabriel as Michael cautiously headed the party. Raphael brought up the rear, soldier-tense.

"Where are your parents?" he asked, gingerly sitting on a wooden chair. The single armchair in the room had far too many springs sticking out to be safe. The other three settled on the couch, trying to avoid similar problems. Evelyn frowned at him as she carelessly plopped herself on the armchair. The tray landed on the rickety table, jug sloshing and glasses rattling.

"Don't have any. I was in the system. Ran away from my last foster family, found this place. It's not exactly five stars, but it's shelter." She busied herself with the juice, measuring out five glasses and distributing them without making eye contact.

"Aren't you lonely?" Carmen asked softly.

Evelyn snorted. Gabriel tilted his head at her.

"You've always been lonely." Her head snapped up. "Always something different about you, separating you from normal people. You never felt a part of humanity." He leaned forward, ignoring Carmen's panicked looks and his brothers' neutral ones. "Am I right?"

"I was in foster care," Evelyn said coldly.

"So were we, but that's not what I meant, and you know it." Gabriel rolled the glass between his palms, watching the liquid swish back and forth rather than their host. "How are your nightmares?"

Silence.

"Get out."

"Wait, Ms. Smyth—" Michael began.

"I said get out!" She stood, furious. "I don't need doctors, I don't need help—"

"We need help," Raphael cut in. "*Your* help. And we weren't hired by doctors, or kids sent to persuade you to go back into the system."

"Our best friends are missing. Their brother," Carmen nodded to the Elohims, "and my sister in all but blood. They are in danger, and you may be their only chance. Please."

"What can *I* do?" Evelyn asked.

"You are God," Michael said quietly. "You can stop the angels from ending the world."

Evelyn stared at him, then looked down and drained her glass.

"I'll go make us some coffee."

Chapter Fourteen

Ariel peeked around the door to the Sheriff's office, the lamp light bleeding out of the room providing the only illumination in the shadows of the station. Bill Reed hunched over his desk, paperwork piled beside him and gun belt slung over the back of his chair with his jacket. She smiled slightly at the sight before rapping her knuckles once on the door.

"Boss?"

He looked up, bloodshot eyes peering at her. "Is it time to go?"

"Just about, boss." She stepped into the room, the form clutched in her hands. "It's late. But I was wondering if you could do something for me first."

"You finally taking that leave?"

She blinked. "How did you—?"

"I've been nagging you for weeks, and you've been getting antsy these past couple of days. Something happen?"

"Not…exactly." Ariel handed him the leave request form, watching him scribble out his signature as she elaborated. "More like, something might happen, and I want to be prepared."

"Well, you're approved," Bill said gruffly. "And Ariel?"

She looked back at him, slowly pulling on her jacket. "Yes?"

"You know we're here for you, right? You say the word, and we'll help you with anything you need," he said, shifting uncomfortably. Emotion was never the Sheriff's strong suit.

She nodded gratefully at him, knowing she would never take him up on his offer. The kind of help she needed, humans couldn't give. After all, even with all their power at their disposal, Wiccans barely escaped an angelic battle with their lives intact, let alone limb and mind. She wouldn't risk her fragile mortal friends in this war if she could help it, even if some of them did have unusual talents.

Now she had to go find the other archangels and make sure they weren't as suicidal as Lucifer seemed to be. Honestly, they were the eldest; shouldn't they have a better sense of self-preservation?

Kali hung up the phone, not bothering to say goodbye. None of her contacts could tell her anything, or get any information out of their contacts. They couldn't even get her access to the Ministry of Defence; at least the government would be able to limit the angel's abuse of human resources.

Of course, she wouldn't tell the government about the angels or the Apocalypse. She would simply heavily imply that the albino one was part of a terrorist cell. Everyone was twitchy about terrorists these days.

She got up from her desk chair and paced around her private study. Anthony never came in here; this was her space, her temple, just as the basement was his sanctuary. They lived together as a married couple, but their romantic relationship remained on paper. Anthony had been enlisted by his God as she had been, for the sole purpose of guarding His precious archangels.

Kali hadn't asked why the archangels needed protection, or why He asked her to help. She just wanted to be a mother again, and with her power fading a little more each day, it seemed like a good idea at the time. Granted, it wasn't quite the chore she expected it to be, but it also wasn't how she envisioned her future as a goddess.

She came to a stop in front of her altar, lighting the incense and breathing the smoke as it drifted up. The three archangels had left with their human friend to find God early this morning, and Anthony and Willow had gone back to the police to see if they had found anything else. Kali doubted it—they were only human, after all—but they all needed to do something to feel like they were helping their charges.

A faint knock at the front door had her frowning and dousing the incense. The neighbours knew by now not to come around and bother her family or Willow's; most likely it was some official, but she took the altar matches with her just in case. Worst case scenario, she could light a fire and order it to attack any threats while she escaped. She cursed once again that her power wasn't as strong as it used to be; in the old days, Kali could have wreathed herself in a fire of her own essence and none would have been able to penetrate it.

She locked the study door behind her and walked silently to the front door. Whoever it was started knocking again, the sounds quicker and louder than before. Evidently the annoying person thought this was an urgent matter.

Kali opened the door, ready to berate the visitor for disrupting her. Her ire dimmed slightly when she registered the black police uniform, but spiked sharply into fear when she finally understood just what was standing at her door.

"What do *you* want?" the goddess spat at the angel, barely stopping herself from burning it—her—alive.

"I need to speak to the archangels," the angel said tersely, eyeing Kali warily. "Are they here?"

"No," she snapped. "Now leave, before I find myself with a bothersome pile of ashes on my front porch."

The angel blinked, then smiled wryly. "I take it you've already had the pleasure of meeting Uriel and his mercenaries."

"Not personally," she said, still refusing to change her stance. "He has attacked my family several times, however, and it is not the best first impression Heaven could make."

The angel snorted. "No kidding. I'm Ariel, by the way."

Kali raised an eyebrow. "Pleasure. Go exist elsewhere now." She began to shut the door, glaring fiercely when Ariel forced it back open. Her hand twitched towards the matches.

"Please, where did they go?" Ariel asked. "I need to find them before Uriel does; he's determined to bring them back home and 'rehabilitate' them." The scorn in Ariel's voice made Kali pause and take a closer look at the angel. The anger and derision tasted like hot iron and crabapples on her tongue, layered over the brine of grief. But there, under everything, was the faintest trace of honey.

"Wait here," she told the angel, retreating back into the house. Kali deliberated for a moment, then returned to her study. She knelt down in front of the altar, taking an old iron disc that had once been a candle holder from the shelf. The goddess dipped her finger in the incense oil, unaffected by the heat, and carefully outlined the shape of an eye in the middle of the amulet. She stood and grabbed a length of leather cord from her desk, using a touch of power to bore a hole at the top of the disk.

Kali opened the door fully this time, but still blocked the doorway with her body. "Here," she said brusquely, handing the completed amulet to the angel. "Show this to your enemies, and it will curse them. It won't kill them unless they attack you, but it will give them pause; enough for you to get away."

"Thank you," Ariel breathed, taking the eye delicately. "I'll pass it on to the Wiccan when I find her; she will use it better than I."

Kali nodded and stepped back. "Angel," she called. "Take care of our family."

Ariel smiled and nodded back, fisting a hand over her heart. Kali rolled her eyes and shut the door, locking it and activating her own small wards.

She had a lot of work to do.

"How did you come to this conclusion again?" Evelyn asked Carmen, one eyebrow raised in disbelief.

"Well, I kind of figured out the whole archangel thing first," she explained, waving a hand at the brothers. "Or, well, Ro probably did, but she's not here, so…yeah," Carmen added sheepishly.

"And then Carmel did her computer thing and we found you," Gabriel finished brightly.

"Right," Evelyn said slowly.

"Ms. Smyth," Raphael began.

"Call me Evelyn, honestly. Even if I am God, we are the same age. None of this honorific business."

"Right," Raphael said hesitantly. "Well, if we could just—"

The front windows blew inward as the door splintered and crumbled. Six figures burst in, wielding blades and looking entirely too indifferent. The albino wasn't among them, but Carmen was absolutely sure he had something to do with this. He seemed just like the sort of coward that would send assassins and not come to see the job done himself.

"Oh, this is just fantastic," Raphael grumbled, before he was tackled by a particularly burly angel.

Carmen found herself shoved behind Gabriel, barely catching a glimpse of Michael leaping to Raphael's aid before—

The entire room was soaked in water. Their attackers screamed, flesh smoking and fading from view, though the level of damage seemed to vary. One Korean man simply stood there in shock before abruptly vanishing. The others were not so lucky, and barrelled out of the house as more of their bodies melted away.

Carmen leaned around Gabriel, who was still planted protectively in front of her, and eyed Evelyn speculatively. The other woman let the hose drop to the floor sheepishly, shrugging at their expressions.

"I…may have had a priest bless my pipes when the dreams started," she admitted.

Michael blinked. "That's…a really good idea. Why didn't we do that?"

"How are angels affected by holy water?" Carmen wondered. "Wouldn't it just be like splashing a human with normal water?"

"Anything unholy—not following the will of God—burns on contact with holy water," Raphael explained.

"I don't follow God's will, and holy water doesn't burn me," Carmen pointed out.

"Humans aren't affected," Gabriel amended. "Fallen angels, demons, monsters—those with magic or an unholy core react badly to the purity of holy water. Most of those pricks were disobedient, but with no one to cast them out of heaven they've been allowed to run free."

Carmen rolled her eyes at his grave tone. "Yeah, okay. As long as they stop attacking us, I don't really care what makes it work."

"We should head back home," Michael said, turning towards the near demolished front of the house. He froze.

"I don't think that is advisable," a smooth voice said from what was left of the doorway. Uriel picked his way through the rubble, flanked by two other angels. Raphael tensed and moved in front of Evelyn, while Gabriel did the same for Carmen. Michael stepped forward, swallowing nervously but lifting his chin stubbornly.

"We can't have you putting yourselves in danger, now, can we?" the angel asked pleasantly. Michael narrowed his eyes and said nothing. Uriel sighed. "Must you refuse to be reasonable? Perhaps it would best if you came with us—for your own safety, of course."

"Full of shit as ever, Uriel."

A woman dressed as a small town deputy emerged from the kitchen. Very deliberately, she placed herself between the teens and the angels, unflinching in the glacier sights of the other man. He chuckled humorously.

"Ariel," he sneered. "And here I thought Heaven had put down all the traitorous riffraff."

"You're still running around, aren't you? Clearly the exterminators need to be replaced."

The two of them were perfectly still, amiable from afar, though tension was visible in every line of their bodies. The angels accompanying Uriel twitched restlessly behind him.

"What do you hope to accomplish here, Ariel?" he sighed. "Surely you don't plan to fight us? We'd kill you in a heartbeat."

"I'm not stupid," Ariel replied. "But I still have my faith, and I'm willing to die for it." She held up a small talisman, half the size of her palm, dangling from a long leather cord.

Uriel's eyes widened. "You wouldn't."

"Wouldn't I?" Her tone never wavered, her hands and gaze steady. "How far are you willing to go, Uriel? Are you willing to risk everything?"

He hesitated, staring fearfully at the amulet. It was enough.

With a strong gust of wind, and the wet tear of wings through the fabric of reality, Ariel had disappeared.

And so had the five children.

Uriel screamed.

☆

Evelyn and Carmen stumbled upon landing, unused to angel flight. The brothers fared a little better, though their balance was thrown off by their lack of wings. Ariel, of course, looked like she had just gone for a walk.

"Where are we?" Michael growled, eyes narrowed suspiciously at Ariel. She ignored him, carefully stepping forward as if she were testing something.

"Hey!" Carmen had regained her bearings. "Who are you, anyway?"

"My name is Ariel," she said shortly, not taking her attention away from the space in front of her. "This is where it's supposed to be; come on, you let me in before."

"What?" Evelyn asked, glancing nervously at the others to see if they understood the angel. She wasn't reassured.

"Great," Gabriel sniped. "Of all the angels that could rescue us, we got the one driven insane by human life."

"I am not insane," Ariel said reproachfully. "There is a bunker here, though it appears to be hidden once more—"

A high pitched noise, rather like the wheels of a train squealing on the tracks as they braked, preceded two human-shaped missiles slamming into the brothers and Carmen. Evelyn and Ariel stared at each other uncertainly, wondering if they should intercede.

"Stars above, what *took* you so long?" Ro asked thickly, face buried in Carmen's neck. Luce was currently being squashed by his brothers.

"I didn't know we were on a deadline," Michael said, refusing to let go of the limbs he had claimed.

"Yeah, really, Ro; you couldn't have left us a clue or something?" Gabriel chipped in. He and Raphael had each latched on to other parts of Lucifer's body, and didn't seem inclined to relinquish him any time soon.

"As touching as this reunion is," Ariel drawled. "Could we maybe move this inside?"

Ro jerked back, face darkening as she met Ariel's gaze. "*You*!"

"Me," she said calmly. "Now—"

"You're an angel?" Ro's voice was steadily rising. She clambered to her feet, her friends hastily following as she advanced on the deputy.

"I am," Ariel said, not backing down at Ro's fury. The others couldn't help but be impressed at the angel's audacity.

"What do you want with us?" Ro demanded, clearly in full defence mode for her friends.

"To help you," Ariel stated simply. She held up a hand to forestall Ro's protests. "I am not like the other angels you have encountered; not even close. There are some of us who still believe in the old order, who believe that Heaven is corrupted and the archangels were unjustly accused and driven apart. Uriel has twisted many of the lesser angels with his new power and rank, and the ones born after the war did not know any better. Few of us survived that have the same mindset as myself."

"So what?" Ro asked angrily. "You expect us to believe that you want everything to go back to the way it was and hope you can fix everything?"

"I have no illusions that I can do anything of significance on my own," Ariel said shortly, finally growing impatient with Ro's attitude. "But you lot are game changers. You could bring the armies of Heaven and Hell to their knees; perhaps even restore the archangels and God."

"God?"

"Hell?"

Ro and Carmen spoke in perfect sync, turning confused gazes on each other. The brothers just rolled their eyes, while the other two women looked rather bemused.

"Can we go inside now? Getting a little nervous out here," Gabriel proclaimed, glancing around nervously. The sun was beginning to set, making way for the shadows to creep between the trees. Indeed, now that the group had fallen silent, they noticed the hushed darkness crawling in from all sides.

"Inside is good," Luce agreed, leading the way into the bunker. Without the distraction of reunion, the tension once more thickened between himself and Ro.

"Right," Michael began, closing the door after him. "It appears we all have a lot of catching up to do. Who wants to go first?"

Awkward looks were exchanged, Ro eventually sighing and sitting down on her favourite chair. "We've been busy looking for solutions here, as I assume you already guessed. The whole thing with the memories—" She broke off and glanced at the brothers, continuing when they nodded in affirmation. "That was me. I was just trying to do it for Luce, although apparently I overpowered it a bit."

"You can restore memories?" Evelyn asked curiously, a thread of hope winding its way through her voice. Ro nodded, frowning slightly as she examined the newcomer.

"We found God," Carmen explained. Gabriel rolled his eyes as Ro just shrugged and went with it.

"Fine. I might be able to help you," she told Evelyn. "It will probably take some time, though. I have to get more supplies, and most likely it will take a lot more power."

Evelyn smiled gratefully. Ro surged on, suddenly wanting to get this over with as soon as possible. "I was looking for a spell to trap angels in Hell, like what happened to Lucifer according to the Bible. I found one, and while it was only partially translated, it seemed to have what I needed. Turns out, it was more about releasing those that deviate from God rather than trapping them."

The room was quiet for a long moment. Carmen got up and joined Ro in the chair, comforting her as she broke down. Luce felt guilt and pain rip through him, knowing that this was what he should have done days ago. Ro was under just as much stress as he was—more, considering the pressure she was putting herself under.

And he hadn't exactly been going easy on her, either. Always expecting her to fix things and conjure up a miracle—something he knew perfectly well was extremely rare and almost impossible to pull off, even for an angel—it was a wonder she had held up thus far.

"If it makes you feel any better, Ariel scared the piss out of Uriel," Gabriel offered. Ro let out a wet and broken laugh, eyeing the angel with new appreciation.

"Is that so?" Ariel smiled, soft but still slightly strained.

"I wouldn't go that far. I was able to distract him long enough to get this lot out of there."

"That's not what I saw," Raphael objected. "Something you did frightened him."

"You threatened him with something; what was it?" Michael asked.

"A Lady Gaga CD?" Luce jumped in innocently.

Carmen made a strangled little sound, and then they were all in hysterics. Ariel just looked confused, proving that for all she had adapted to human life, she was still something *other*. Even Evelyn was amused.

"It was a talisman," Ariel told them, evidently deciding to nip their foolishness in the bud—which was absurd, in Luce's humble opinion. They needed a good laugh.

"What kind of talisman?" Ro's curiosity for all things magical was obviously peaked.

"I got it from a pagan, before I went to find your friends," Ariel explained, tilting her head. "Would you like to see it?"

"Um…*yes*." She looked ecstatic when Ariel handed it over, handling it like glass. "This is a Hindu evil eye, right?"

Ariel inclined her head regally, slipping back into the refined mannerisms of angels around Ro. Luce mused on the reasons behind that as Ro frowned and flipped the amulet in her hands. "This symbol at the centre…Bhavatarini?"

"The annihilator of evil things, yes. I thought it was appropriate, and she had a vested interest in helping me," Ariel said.

"She?" Gabriel asked.

"Kali," Ariel said mildly, clearly not understanding the gravity of her statement.

"Kali?" Lucifer yelped, exchanging shocked glances with his brothers. The girls rolled their eyes.

"Yes, Kali," Ariel said impatiently. "Are you going to repeat everything I say?"

"But—"

"Kali's the actual goddess, and Anthony is one of the disciples of God—a very devoted priest that had been brought back from Heaven, probably to watch over you. Didn't you know?" Ro asked, laughter threatening to rise again.

The Elohims gaped at her. "How do *you* know this?" Ariel asked, as the boys were apparently incapable of speaking.

"We're Wiccans," she huffed. "Grandmother knew who Kali was immediately, and she pestered Anthony until he told her what he was and how he got here. Also, I eavesdropped," Ro added sheepishly. Luce snorted.

"Of course you did," he said fondly, smiling hesitantly as she met his gaze. *I'm sorry; I don't want to lose you. Are we good?*

"Like you've never done it," Ro scoffed, rolling her eyes in mock exasperation. *I'm sorry too; I can't lose you either. We're good.*

"Right," Carmen said, amused. "Now that you two have kissed and made up, with a disturbing amount of kissing, can we move on?"

"There was no kissing!" Luce protested.

"That's her point, bro," Gabriel snickered. Lucifer sulked.

"I should go back to the station," Ariel declared, standing and brushing her uniform free of imaginary dust. Ro glanced up in surprise.

"You're leaving already? Oh, here, your talisman—"

Ariel shook her head, already moving towards the door. "You will use it better than I would; as you said earlier, you are a Wiccan. Pagan magicks will work for you more than they ever will a Judeo-Christian angel." She gave a short little wave before vanishing.

"Huh," Ro murmured, staring down at the trinket. Carmen looked at the others in exasperated amusement. Michael and Raphael smirked at each other and stood, stretching.

"I assume you two have a place for us to sleep?" Michael asked, looking pointedly at Luce. He rolled his eyes and nodded, leading his brothers to the lower barracks. Evelyn glanced between the girls and the Elohims before following the boys downstairs.

"Come on, I'll help you move your stuff downstairs, since no one else bothered to help," Ro offered. She raised an eyebrow and grinned when Carmen groaned.

"We left the Astra in Edinburgh."

Ro's grin widened.

"It had all our stuff in it! Michael's going to be *pissed*."

Ro's laughter bounced off the walls, ringing through the bunker and bringing smiles to the others. For tonight, at least, they could let go of a little of their worry. They were back together and stronger than ever.

Chapter Fifteen

Kali woke suddenly, staring at the shadowed ceiling. On the opposite side of the king bed, Anthony muttered something and turned away from her. She stretched out her senses, trying to find what had disrupted her sleep.

It didn't take long.

The faint click of toenails was accompanied by a bass growl, almost out of the human range of hearing. Kali held herself perfectly still as the hellhound prowled down the hall to their room. The goddess didn't have to see the monster to know it was hunting her and Anthony specifically; a hellhound would only dare to hunt a deity if it was ordered to.

She reached out and grasped Anthony's shoulder, waking him instantly. He started to say something, but fell silent abruptly as the door swung slowly open, revealing the abomination.

The beast was skeletal, matted fur clinging to bone. Its body was covered in open wounds and weeping sores, and the pads of its feet cracked and bled.

Kali was going to have the entire house cleaned after this.

Its lips peeled back from its dagger-like teeth, ropes of saliva dripping from the sides of its mouth. The floor smoked where drops landed, small holes burning through the wood.

Forget cleaning. She would just burn down the house and move instead. Possibly all the way back to India.

The hound's milky, dead eyes bulged out of its head. It couldn't see them, but its ragged ears cocked in their direction, and it heaved in air to pinpoint their position.

It would only give them a few seconds to act, until it was certain of its attack. Luckily, a few seconds were all she needed.

The henna she had inked onto her hands after the angel had left burned as she met the hound's lunge with her palms. The evil eyes at the centre of each palm glowed with fierce fire when they came into contact with the abomination. It writhed under her fingers, letting out a shrieking howl as flesh turned to ash.

The instant the hellhound was gone, Kali leapt out of bed towards the closet. Grabbing a pair of combats, socks, and a tee for both of them, she came back into the bedroom to find Anthony sorting through their weapons case. She changed quickly, setting Anthony's clothes aside; they were more dressed down than they usually preferred, but functionality would be more useful at the moment.

Anthony tossed her a belt and two sheathed daggers, changing his own clothes and strapping a short sword to his back. Kali fitted two cuffs around her wrists, snapping them closed and activating the battle sigils. He simply hung his silver cross pendant around his neck once more.

As ready for battle as they would ever be, the two protectors headed out into the fray.

Carmen walked into the living room three days later, clutching a warm mug and practicing her amazing talent of being able to see through her eyelashes. She stumbled to a stop at the gigantic chalk pentagram inscribed on the floor, Ro spinning around in the middle like a demented spider.

"It's too early for this," Carmen mumbled retreating back to the relative safety of the kitchen.

Relative because Gabriel had decided to try cooking again.

"You do remember the last time you tried this, right?" Carmen asked, voice still thick with sleep. Gabriel pouted at her.

"You wound me! I can fix pancakes," he grumbled.

"Where did you even get this stuff? I was under the impression we couldn't just pop down to the shops," Michael remarked, wandering into the room and stealing a slice of strawberry. Gabriel smacked at his hands.

"Ariel brought it up. Said we weren't taking care of ourselves properly," Raphael answered, towel hanging around his shoulders and only dressed in a pair of trousers. Any awkwardness they might have felt around seeing each other in a less than decent state was eradicated fairly early on in their acquaintance. At this point, Carmen was only uncomfortable around Gabriel. Ro and Luce had also taken great pains recently to avoid being in the vicinity of each other when there was a chance their mutual feelings could come to light.

Times like these brought into sharp relief just how idiotic her friends could be.

"Ariel's here?" Carmen asked, momentarily distracting Gabriel, who was trying to salvage his blackened pancake. At least, it was blackened on one side. The other was sickly pale and dripping and oozing whatever the hell Gabriel had decided to fill it with.

"Yes, she is," Raphael said, watching as Michael confiscated the spatula. Gabriel's protests were refuted by his older brother's firm assertions that 'he was never allowed near a kitchen again, nor anything remotely resembling cooking materials, or even food unless he was intending to eat it and he was only allowed to do unnatural things to it if it wouldn't cause fatal food poisoning and Gabriel would eat it all.'

Gabriel went into the living room to sulk.

Luce and Evelyn entered, peering around blearily. They were followed by Ariel, who had obviously taken it upon herself to get them out of bed. She blinked at the destruction of her foodstuffs, unused to Gabriel's brand of cooking.

"Breakfast will take a little longer, seeing as Gabriel got to the kitchen before anyone else," Michael informed them apologetically. Luce smirked and nodded, while the other girls just exchanged confused looks.

"What's Ro doing?" Carmen asked, hoping one of the boys would know.

"She said she was going to try and retrieve my memories today," Evelyn piped up. Carmen tilted her head, not alone in her worry.

"Should she be doing this so soon after the whole," Luce waved a hand in the air, "Hell thing?" Michael frowned at him.

"We have to trust she knows what she's doing, Lucifer," he rebuked. "How much do you know about Wiccan magic?"

Luce ducked his head sheepishly, finally acknowledging that he was next to useless in matters like these. Archangels they might once have been, but that didn't mean they knew everything. The opposite, really, especially when it concerned pagans and their ilk. This was why the archangels needed to stick together: they balanced each other out. Luce had been off-kilter ever since Michael left the first time, even though they hadn't remembered their Heavenly lives at the time.

"He has a point," Ariel chipped in. "Retrieving the memories of archangels with full power stores is one thing; restoring those of God while weak due to performing several major spells in quick succession is quite another."

Carmen took a moment to pick that sentence apart before shaking her head stubbornly. "Ro's strong, and if she thinks she can do this, then we have to have faith she is smart enough not to kill herself. We'll at least be there if something goes wrong."

"Carmen's right," Raphael said. "Ro is stubborn, and nothing we say is going to deter her at this point. We will just have to be conscious of her safety when she refuses to be."

"Great," Luce said. "Do any of you know magickal Wiccan first aid?"

"Shut up, Lucifer," Carmen snapped. She stalked out into the living room where Ro was busy terrorizing Gabriel into doing…something for her. Carmen didn't really want to know.

"Carmen! Good, you can stand at the Water point and hold the aloe," Ro said, herding her over to the pentagram and plopping a bowl in her hands. "Will the rest of you get in here? Except for Ariel; no offence, but I don't want you around while I'm working pagan magicks. You get nervous, which makes me nervous, which—"

"Gets us all blown up," Lucifer finished cheerfully, taking the bowl of…plant (Ro called it cinquefoil, whatever that meant) and allowing her to position him how she wanted.

Carmen smirked at her brain's phrasing.

"Michael, you get the Dragon's Blood, go stand on the point by the door—not that one, the *front* door, yes—Raphael, you hold the caraway over there. Gabriel, stop sulking and stand still. And do *not* disturb the cloves. Especially once they are lit. Now," Ro turned to Evelyn, ignoring Gabriel's panicked squawks and Lucifer's taunts. "You did drink the tea last night? Good; you need to sit in the centre of the pentagram, there, legs folded; refresh the eyebright on your lids, and then don't move."

She strode out of the circle, taking deep breaths to steady herself. "Right. Once the spell is in progress, there is no backing out. If anyone is getting cold feet, let me know now."

Silence. Ro made sure Ariel was gone and nodded sharply. "Okay then. Let's get started, shall we?" She circled clockwise, lighting the bowls as she went, finally coming back to Michael. She began speaking in what Carmen presumed to be Gaelic, although there was a strange accent to it she had never heard before.

The power literally crackled in the air, electricity arcing across the walls and the pentagram. The flames leapt from the bowls, mimicking the encircled star above their heads. Luce's breath caught in his chest, almost choking as phantom dirt coated his mouth and throat. The others seemed to be suffering similar effects, though Luce had the sneaking suspicion that each person was the victim of the element they were personifying.

Ro kept chanting, circling at the same steady pace.

The pentagram of fire began spinning in the air, nearly singeing their hair on a few occasions. They didn't dare flinch, all too aware of Ro's warnings.

Evelyn wasn't moving. She wasn't even breathing.

Luce wondered if he had been like this, if there was some sign that it was working.

Her eyes snapped open. Her pupils and irises were gone; in fact, Evelyn's eyes were entirely orbs of glowing white-gold swirls. She tilted her head back, opened her mouth, and *screamed*. The sound was entirely inhuman.

The room exploded.

The fire expanded so fast it blew all of them off their feet, bowls clattering to the floor in a shower of sparks and embers and ash, Evelyn crumpling in the middle and Ro somehow the only one still standing, albeit a trifle unsteadily.

A ghostly apparition stood in front of the Wiccan, evaluating Ro without saying a word. Maybe it couldn't. It—she—reached a hand forward and brushed a hand down the Wiccan's cheek before the vision faded away.

Luce blinked, wondering if that had been an afterimage from the explosion. Although, it looked far too much like Evelyn—except older and dressed like royalty and had an air that announced her importance to the universe—to be anything his brain could come up with. Or be normal, for that matter. Of course, he was friends with Ro; when had things ever been normal with her?

Not that he was complaining. Up until recent events, normal had been entirely too boring of a concept.

He kind of wished for normal, now.

Ro let out a shaky breath, immediately going to Evelyn's side. Luce picked himself up off the floor, noticing his brothers doing the same. Gabriel went to Carmen's side to check on her, but no one seemed seriously hurt by the random magical fire.

Apart from Evelyn, who wasn't waking up.

"Luce, give me hand, will you? I want to put her in the first floor quarters. Oh, and someone needs to tell Ariel she can come back." Ro lifted Evelyn gently, Luce supporting her head while Raphael opened the doors and cleared the floor of their things. Ro chewed her lip worriedly as she tucked the human incarnation of God into her old bed, casting a few monitoring and diagnostic charms on her as she did so. They didn't tell Ro anything besides the state of consciousness Evelyn was in—which Ro could have figured out with her eyes, thank you very much.

"I'll keep the monitoring charms up, so if she wakes, we'll know," Ro said softly, slipping out behind Luce and gently closing the door. "Once Ariel gets here she can bunk with Evelyn, so someone will be on hand that has more power and experience to deal with this."

"It's not your fault, Ro," Luce reassured her. He'd already harmed their relationship by blaming Ro before; he wasn't about to do it again. A fresh wave of guilt crested over him as he recalled the deterioration Ro had gone through after the 'whole hell thing.' Barely eating or sleeping, Ro had tended to avoid him, though he had done the same to her. With his brothers and Carmen here, she'd been getting better, but the damage had been done.

"You were right, I wasn't ready," she sighed. "I should have rested more, prepared better; I overestimated my abilities and the limits of the spell, and we are extremely lucky things turned out as well as they did."

"You heard that?" Luce asked, still stuck on the beginning of Ro's confession.

Her lips quirked. "Open floor plan, Luce. The door was wide open, and sound carries from one room to another; it would have been harder to ignore you."

"Ah," he said, embarrassed.

"Quite," she said dryly. Raised voices reached them from the front room, and they quickened their pace.

Ariel was irate, clearly furious that they potentially damaged God and didn't bother to have her on hand. She turned on Ro as soon as they stepped into the room.

"Are you *insane*?" she spat, nearly frothing at the mouth. Luce bristled.

"Probably," Ro said instantly. Yeah, Luce could tell that wasn't helping at all.

"If you've broken Her—"

"Hey!" Luce moved forward, chin jutted forward defensively. "Evelyn knew the risks, and Ro did her best. If you don't like how things turned out, maybe you should have offered an alternative!" He glared at her, mildly shocked when Ariel immediately backed down.

Well, at least he hadn't lost too much of his touch. He'd always been good at intimidating the fledglings.

Michael was glaring at him. Right, he didn't like it when Lucifer bullied the little ones. Although, sometimes he was too soft on them. The quicker they learned to stand up and defend themselves, especially to the ones hardest to face, the better off the young angels would be.

Lucifer had three older brothers fighting his battles for him. Maybe that's why things ended the way they did. He didn't know how to stand up for what was right, and so he fell down instead.

When did he get so *maudlin*? He was blaming Gabriel. When in doubt, always blame Gabriel.

Ariel tossed a copy of *The Guardian* at them. Luce frowned as he caught it, shaking it open and freezing. His hands trembled as he stared at the front page.

"What is this?" he whispered, feeling his family gathering around him.

"It came in this morning," Ariel said, voice flat. Several gasps were let out from the teens as they saw the headline 'SCOTLAND BORDERS TOWN MASSACRED OVERNIGHT' over a picture of Kelso before they had left.

'*List of dead on 3A.*' Lucifer ripped the paper open to the correct page, eyes flicking frantically down the names. So many people they knew were on there, kids from school, neighbours, teachers, people they walked past every day. Kali and Anthony weren't on there, as far as Luce could see, but in the middle of the F's—

Charlie Feye

Jasmine Feye

Willow Fitzgerald

Luce felt Ro's agony seconds before Michael tore the paper from his hands. He spun to hold her, refusing to let go even as she beat against his chest with fists and what little reserves of magic she had left. Gabriel could be heard desperately trying to console Carmen, but both girls were rapidly descending into frenzied states.

Abruptly, the cacophony was silenced by Ariel. She pressed a hand to each of their foreheads, sending them into a deep sleep. It wouldn't be a natural rest, but it would serve its purpose just as well.

He still glared at her for using magic on Ro.

Luce and Gabriel took their girls to the barracks, leaving Michael to show Ariel where she would be staying for the night, even though it was only a few hours past breakfast.

It was amazing his internal clock hadn't broken yet, considering the bashing it was constantly receiving.

This was going to be a long night.

Ro knew she was dreaming.

This was nowhere she'd ever seen before, and yet the peace that filled her gave her an idea as to where she had been summoned to.

Because there was no doubt she had been summoned, not with the being currently standing in front of her.

God, now known as Evelyn Smyth, smiled gently at one of Her favourites. Yes, she was a Wiccan, and practised pagan magicks, and was from questionable origin. So what? Rowan Fitzgerald had watched over and protected Her most precious children when She couldn't. It was the work of a saint.

Somehow, God didn't think Rowan would appreciate being compared to a saint.

"You aren't Evelyn," she said, eyeing God warily.

God raised an eyebrow. "Aren't I?"

Ro frowned at Her. "So that's where Ariel gets it from...and no. You aren't. Evelyn hasn't remembered her past, even if she does know of it, nor has she regained her powers. Of course, since supreme monotheistic Gods are omniscient, You easily could have travelled from anywhen to speak with me. The question is: Why?"

God threw back Her head and laughed. "Oh, you are *a clever one! It's good to know my sons are in good hands with you."*

Ro rolled her eyes. "I think Gabe is more in Carmen's hands than mine."

God hummed. "Perhaps, but a good choice nonetheless. Especially considering that girl's heritage."

Ro stared at the celestial being, and then shook her head. "Whatever, I don't even want to know. I would like You to tell me what You are doing in my dreams."

God sighed and waved Her hand, conjuring two seats hewn from what looked like redwood stumps. In fact, they seemed to be in a clearing of redwoods. "Please, sit. I cannot stay long, but you need to know certain things."

"Okay," Ro said, gingerly settling herself in the deep seat. "What things?"

"First of all, you can break the spell holding My memories back; Ariel will help you restore Me," God said warmly. "Once you have done that, you need to ask Me about the Hitgalut Ritual. I'll make it worth your while, promise."

"Right," Ro said slowly. "Any other gold nuggets of wisdom?"

"He loves you, you know," She said softly, smiling as Ro looked at Her sharply. "Instead of seeing what you expect to see, look

beneath the surface and listen to what he's telling you every moment of every day."

Ro struggled to bring enough air into her lungs, thinking for one panicked second that she was suffocating as the edges of her vision went black. But no, she was just waking up.

"Oh, and Ro? Tell your friend that her parents are with your family, and they are cheering you all on," God called after her as she began to surface.

Ro yelped and fell out of her new bed. Next to her, Carmen grumbled and pulled the blanket over her head as she rolled over. Ro groaned and pulled herself up.

Why did this always happen to them?

It was another two days before Ro was able to corner Ariel in Evelyn's room. They sat at her bedside, not looking at one another and both fretting over the girl lying before them. Eventually Ariel spoke, shyly offering an olive branch. Ro wondered if her boys had threatened the angel.

"Finally get some breathing room?"

Ro groaned, Ariel chuckling lightly at the hunted expression on the Wiccan's face. "When we were about seven, I broke my arm because some idiot dared me to climb the tallest tree on the playground as high as I could, I was an idiot who took him up on it, and I fell fifteen feet to the ground." Ariel winced. "The boys mothered me for *weeks*. I thought that was as bad as they could get. I was wrong."

"The archangels have always been…overly cautious with the rest of our safety. I think it's just an older brother thing," Ariel told her. The two of them shared a rueful grin.

"She won't wake up," Ariel said, returning her focus to the woman on the bed. "As far as I can tell, there's nothing wrong with her, nothing that should be keeping her like this, she's just…waiting."

"I dreamt of God," Ro said slowly. Ariel's head snapped up. "She told me that I can restore Her, that you can help me help Her. I think…I think that means we try again, except the spell would have to be even more powerful this time. It's sort of like, the first time only got halfway done before it was forced to stop by whatever safety measures She put in place to start with, and now we have to complete the circuit. You know?"

"Not really," Ariel said honestly. "But if it's power you need..." She hesitated, gathering her courage, and then plunged on. "Sacrifices always make magic more powerful. Blood, soul, life...all of it, and the more willing, the better." Her shoulders drew back, chin lifting proudly. "If this will help fix my family, and my home, then I am honoured to sacrifice myself for the good of my people; for the good of my Mother." Her gaze fondly rested on Evelyn.

Ro closed her eyes briefly as the power in the words washed over her. That was no idle promise, and as good as binding now.

"They are not going to be pleased," she said, not needing to clarify who she spoke of.

"Perhaps," Ariel answered. "But they cannot stop me, especially considering the nature of it, and we all learned stubbornness at their knees."

Ro laughed shortly. "Yeah, I know the feeling. Alright; it will take a couple of weeks, since I really don't want to screw anything up this time, and I need to recharge anyway, but we'll get your Mother back, Ariel." It was the first time Ro had used the angel's given name, and she smiled at the Wiccan in recognition.

The others wouldn't understand, likely would refuse to listen to reason, but the two girls would defend the decision, and each other. For a time, with a common goal, they united instead of ripping at each other with barely contained hostility. Both of them considered the Elohims family, and by extension knew the other would not hesitate to give up everything if it meant helping them. It was what Ariel was doing now.

"Just in case," Ro said slowly, "let's not give them time to stop us. Don't mention anything about trying the ritual again, or sacrificing yourself, until we're ready, okay?"

"Naturally," Ariel agreed, smiling sadly down at her Mother.

Ro left the angel to her goodbyes.

Chapter Sixteen

"Are you *insane*?"

"Why do people keep asking me that question?" Ro wondered, ignoring Michael's steadily reddening face. The other three brothers were no less angry, though they appeared to be letting Michael take the lead on chewing her out. Carmen looked nervously between the five of them; she always hated it when Ro and the Elohims fought.

Ariel ignored the lot of them, setting up the ritual area and the wooden box she got from…somewhere to contain her Splendour. Life force. Whatever she was willing to give Ro.

"Because it is a legitimate one!" Michael snapped, storming towards her. Ro raised an eyebrow and refused to back down. In all the years they'd known each other, Ro had never backed down. Why did Michael assume she would now?

"Ro," Luce broke in, glancing worriedly at Michael's knotted back. "Isn't this kind of magic…frowned upon in Wiccan culture? I mean—"

"If I were forcibly draining her, yes," Ro said coldly. "But I'm not. Seriously, what is the big deal?"

"The *big deal*?" Raphael exploded. Ro was shocked into silence. She could cut her hands and feet off, and the times Rafe lost his temper would still amount to less than the number of fingers and toes. "The *big deal* is that Splendour is *sacred*, and to take it from someone is the highest crime you can commit. You will kill her, or worse—"

"Enough." Ro's face was blank, and the lack of emotion on her normally expressive face was enough to make him shut up. "One: I'm not an angel, I don't play by your rules, and we are at *war*. Two: Ariel knows the risks; hell, she suggested this bloody spell. Three: She is perfectly willing, which makes all the difference. Ariel called it an honour to do this for her family; if anything, I'm the one who should be freaking honoured. To enable someone to give so much for someone they love and believe in so wholeheartedly? To be able to, in some small way, be a part of that sacrifice? Any Wiccan would pretty much kill themselves to have this chance, and you have no idea what this means for me—for anyone. So until you have a valid reason not to do this: shut up and go stand in your corners."

Ro turned away, effectively dismissing them, and Carmen observed their stricken looks with dismay. She understood both sides here, and both needed a good slap upside the head, but she wished Ro hadn't been quite so harsh on them.

Although, the Elohims should damn well know better than to insult Ro's Wiccan abilities. Seriously, hadn't they learned from the whole period when Luce and Ro fought? Hadn't they had this conversation a million times?

...Okay, so maybe not quite this conversation, but still.

"Once I do this," Ro said quietly to Ariel. "Once I use your...Splendour for the spell, I don't know if it can ever be restored, even by God. You will be stuck as a human, a true human for the rest of your life. And you'll have our lifespan. Are you sure you're okay with that?"

"No," Ariel said. "Which is why you're going to take everything I have. I don't want to keep anything that might give you an extra edge, just for the sake of living a little while longer." She smiled sadly. "I've lived long enough; I'd rather die knowing I made a difference for the people I love."

Ro sighed and shrugged. "Fair enough. This is going to hurt," she added.

"I'm aware. Spells with little to no structure and mostly based on the instincts of the caster and sacrifice usually do. I'm not afraid of a little pain." Ariel gave Ro a sharp, mirthless grin. "Besides, it can't possibly hurt any worse than watching my family tear itself apart."

Ro nodded and settled herself on the couch directly across from the angel. She closed her eyes and held out her hand, palm facing Ariel. Her lip drew between her teeth as her fingers hovered; first over Ariel's forehead, then drifting down to her chest. They paused over her heart—and then lightly pressed down.

The brothers and Carmen were completely unprepared for the severity of Ariel's reaction. Fingers dug into her thighs, nails ripping the cloth. Her back arched, unable to pull away from Ro but trying nonetheless. She tossed her head back, throat convulsing as the angel struggled to pull in air.

Ro reached out with her free hand, pressing down on the lid of the box. The scent of cinnamon and apples wafted through the air as warm gold light leaked out from underneath Ro's fingers. Ariel was clearly struggling to keep silent, but seemed determined not to show any weakness. They had to respect her for that.

It took a couple seconds for the effects of the ritual to register. As Ro drew out Ariel's Splendour, two pairs of amber wings fluttered into existence. Slowly, her skin began to dry and flake, tightening on her bones as her muscles withered. Veins grew more prominent and lost colour with every heartbeat. Feathers began to shed, dropping with increasing speed and vanishing in little flashes of bronze sparks when they hit the floor. Her blond hair began to fall with them, chunks silvering and landing like snow upon the ground. Blue eyes locked with Ro's flaring white-gold ones, pain bleaching the freckles on her face.

It lasted an eternity, and it was over in less than a minute. One moment, Ariel was sitting on the couch physically looking her age, and the next she was just…gone.

And then Ro collapsed. Again.

"You really need to stop doing this to yourself," Luce murmured softly, pressing Ro back onto the mattress when she tried to sit up. "I think you're giving Mike and Rafe a complex."

Ro snorted, closing her eyes in exhaustion. "They'll get over it. It's not like we haven't taken risks before."

"I think they're more worried about the fact that we don't know how to handle this if something goes wrong," Luce said. "Even if they couldn't protect us from the immediate aftermath of our stupidity, Michael and Raphael have always been able to help us through the long-term consequences. They don't know how to do that now; none of us do."

Ro tried to catch his eye, sighing exasperatedly when he refused to look up at her. "Hey. I'm fine. We're going to get through this, and if it bothers you lot that much, I'll teach you which potions and poultices are used for certain ailments; better?"

"I suppose," Luce sighed, put-upon. Ro grinned at his theatrics, receiving a small smile in return. "Oh, by the way, Evelyn woke up for a bit. Raphael went into full mother hen mode and practically poured the broth down her throat."

Ro grimaced, entirely too familiar with Rafe's fierce attitude towards the sick and injured. He was firmly of the opinion that if you were stupid enough to refuse treatment or to not ask for help, you didn't deserve sympathy or mercy. Legendary difficult patients, the ones one heard about on television or in stories from large hospitals in big cities, would quail in the face of Raphael's brand of care.

Luce chuckled. "Yeah, that expression was on every face but Michael's."

"Michael taught Raphael how to be ruthless," Ro grumbled. "Of course he would approve. When am I allowed to get up?"

"I'm under strict orders not to allow you to move until Michael or Raphael approves it."

"Yeah, that's not going to work for me," Ro said. "I can't sit around in bed all day, there's work to be done! Besides, if I knock you out and escape, they can't blame you, right?" She peered at Luce hopefully, pouting when he rolled his eyes and stood.

"I'm going to get Carmen; she wanted a turn when you woke up before they descended."

Ro snorted and waved back as Luce left, leaning back and wondering if there was a Guinness World Record for Most Times Passed Out in a Week.

"Hey, you," Carmen said brightly, slipping into the room. "How are you feeling?"

"I'm fine. Better than I expected, actually. Don't tell the others that," Ro added, wincing. If the brothers understood what could have happened—what usually happened—to the caster during those types of spells, they'd never let her out of the bed again.

"Sure," she said, plopping into Luce's abandoned chair. "So once this whole God remembering thing happens, what are we going to do? Will she fix everything, or…?"

"It's not exactly made for returning powers—not in that sense, anyway," Ro tried to explain. "For a normal human, or for one with powers, like Wiccans, it would allow the person to access their abilities again. For the archangels and God, it's not so much a case of allowing them to access their power as it is—"

"Returning them to their previous species," Carmen finished.

"Right," Ro said. "Which is a whole other area of magic, and should be damn near impossible under the best of circumstances. But they aren't humans that used to be animals, or even twisted human souls that could be redeemed. They are celestial beings, and no one has the power or means to restore them. Simple as that."

"Ro," Carmen sighed. "I hate to break it to you, but nothing is ever simple with you. And for the rest of us mortals, half the words that come out of your mouth make no sense."

"That's discrimination," Ro protested.

"That's honesty," Carmen corrected. "Now, I believe we are about to be ambushed by two very upset Elohim brothers."

Unfortunately, Carmen was right, and not even ten seconds later Michael and Raphael had stalked through the door with grim determination etched on their faces. Ro sighed and waved to Carmen morosely, letting herself be poked and prodded and pestered to the older Elohims' content.

They were going to be unbearable forever after this. Especially about what came next.

"No."

"Michael," Ro sighed.

"*No*," he growled, folding his arms firmly across his chest. "You are not doing that again." Ro's eyes narrowed.

"Michael," Gabriel groaned. "Don't tell Ro she's not going to do something. That's only going to encourage her to spite you."

They ignored him.

"I was visited by God, who told me that I do, in fact, do this again, so I don't think you can exactly stop me," Ro snapped. "Besides, I have to try; we don't have anything better to do, unless you miracled up another solution to our problems."

"Do we really have to be so hostile about this?" Carmen asked wearily.

"Yes," Luce replied promptly. She shot him a dirty look.

"You just woke up from one spell that was incredibly dangerous, and you want to go do another one that's already failed?" Michael asked incredulously. "Forgive me if I'm a little reluctant to let you go kill yourself because you're trying too hard."

"I know my own limits, Michael!"

"Is that why you keep passing out?"

Crack.

Michael's reddening cheek had nothing to do with his own anger, and everything to do with Ro's frustration. His mouth hung open in shock, because Ro used physical violence about as often as Raphael lost his temper. She preferred verbally flaying someone rather than relying on her diminutive strength. Then again, there was a first time for everything.

"Screw you, Michael." Ro's voice was low and tight and furious in a way that only developed recently. Luce remembered their fight after the whole Hell thing as Exhibit A. Come to think of it, that was also right around the time Ro actually started hitting people.

Things had really changed so much if Luce was now the one siding with Ro while Michael naysaid. Or maybe he just trusted Ro more, now.

After all, she had only ever tried to help him and his family; what had he done for her in return? He had no idea why she still went to extreme lengths for them if this is all she got back. Oh, wait; it could possibly have something to do with the fact that she *loved* them.

"I want to do it," Evelyn said quietly from the door, effectively silencing everyone. Except Raphael.

"You shouldn't be out of bed, you need to rest," he said sternly, advancing on the other girl like he was two seconds away from picking her up and throwing her over his shoulder so she couldn't escape. "And you do not need to go through another ordeal like that when you just woke up from the effects of the last one."

"It's my choice," she said, glaring at him. "And I choose to get myself back. I know there's something more to me now, and if I never at least try to find out what it is, then I'll never forgive myself for it."

"She's right," Luce sighed. "I don't like it any more than the rest of you, but it *is* necessary. And it's not like we have a lot of other options here."

Michael scowled. "This shouldn't be an option."

"I trust Ro," Luce replied, locking his gaze with Michael's and not breaking it to see Ro's reaction, even though he so very badly wanted to.

"So do I," Gabriel chipped in. Carmen rolled her eyes at them all.

"Of course I do," she said fondly.

"And I've already trusted her with my life and mind," Evelyn said quietly. "I'll gladly do it again."

"You're all going to get yourselves killed," Raphael grumbled, before sighing heavily. "Fine, fine; someone needs to keep you lot out of trouble."

"Michael?"

Ro wasn't looking at any of them during their declarations of loyalty. Instead she was staring almost fearfully at Michael, as if his vote was the one that would make or break this. Her.

Luce's stomach knotted painfully, and he felt a surge of anger towards his brother.

He most certainly was *not* going to examine that too closely.

Michael looked to Evelyn, trying to make certain this was what she wanted. She held his gaze without flinching, sure of herself. He nodded shortly.

"Okay."

Carmen was beginning to think they should just permanently convert one of the rooms to a spell workspace, because she kind of wanted the living room back for normal living purposes. It was set up almost exactly the same as the last time they did this, with one key difference. Evelyn sat in the centre of the pentagram, the vessel of Ariel's Splendour cradled in her lap. Ro methodically lit the bowls again; Carmen felt a wave of déjà vu slipping over her, and she really hoped this wouldn't end up like the last time.

Ro took a deep breath and began to chant, the barely-familiar words washing over the room. The lilting rhythm probably should have had a more soothing effect, but considering their previous experiences, Carmen was happy she hadn't passed out or dropped the bowl because her palms were soaked in sweat.

In the centre, Evelyn began to glow again.

At Ro's signal, she carefully began unsealing the wax Ro had put around the top of the vessel; releasing Ariel's essence would need delicate timing, or the whole spell could blow up in their faces. Again.

Carmen glanced nervously up at the Fiery Spinning Pentacle of Doom™.

The amber light spilled across the floor, tracing the lines of the pentagram and enveloping Evelyn. It slowly rose to join with the Fiery Spinning Pentacle of Doom™—hoisting Evelyn up with it.

Should that be happening? She would ask Ro. Later. When they weren't in danger of getting blown up. Again.

Okay, so she might be a little panicky. Who could blame her?

That same energy gathered in the air, so cloying she could taste the ozone in the back of her throat. The light intensified, revolving faster and faster and closer and closer and hotter and brighter until—

It imploded. *Again.*

Damn it, Ro.

This time, however, there was no apparition, or backlash of magic. In fact, there was just a lot of smoke, and Carmen took a moment to be grateful that the bunker didn't have fire alarms. They resounded off concrete and steel something awful.

A strong breeze from…somewhere (maybe Ro conjured it) cleared the smoke, allowing it to escape out the door or the toilet or something. They didn't have a chimney, as far as she knew. Evelyn stood blinking in the middle of the room, staring back at all of them.

Carmen wondered what the social etiquette was in this situation. When you meet God after you restored Her memories through a pagan ritual, what do you say? 'Hi?'

Sure. Let's go with that.

"Hi," Carmen said, feeling extremely awkward. God smiled gently at her. "Welcome to Earth?" Why did she say that? It was God, not a freaking alien.

"Carmel's spazzing," Gabriel said gleefully.

"Yes, thank you for that observation, Gabriel," she said tartly, testing if any of Ro's magic had rubbed off enough on her so that she could duct tape his mouth shut. "I'm atheist, and suddenly I'm standing in the same room as God. Piss off."

"You're atheist?" God asked, sounding pretty much the same as before, except with a deeper sense of authority. Also with the sense that She was constantly amused by the universe.

"Yeah. Why?" Carmen asked, really hoping the whole 'not being our religion gets you sent to Hell' thing wasn't true. It wasn't like she didn't believe in God; she just didn't devote herself to one following.

Of course, she was much more likely not to get the VIP access card because of her extracurricular activities, but people always said God works in mysterious ways.

God grinned wider at her, which kind of creeped her out. She was glad God didn't have Her powers so She couldn't read her mind right now. "Nothing significant. Simply an amusing twist of fate. Now," She stretched. "Let's all get some rest, yes?"

"Right," Ro said, blinking rapidly. The boys still seemed stunned into silence. "Trying days, and all that. Rest. Rest is good."

"Yeah," Carmen agreed. "Same sleeping arrangements, then?"

"I don't see why we should change." Ro turned to God. "Rest now, talk later. You coming?" Without waiting for an answer, she headed downstairs. Carmen rolled her eyes and gestured for God to go ahead. The boys seemed frozen to the spot.

"What's up with you lot?" she asked.

"We just invited our Mother to move in with us," Michael said faintly.

Carmen raised an eyebrow. "Not exactly. She's been living with us for a couple weeks, you know."

"Yes, but now She remembers," Gabriel wailed.

"What are you whining about? She's not going to be upset with you; unless you pranked Her before the whole war thing," Carmen said.

"I love how we can be so casual about Heavenly wars and opening Hell," Luce said thoughtfully, moving past Carmen to the stairs. "It won't be that bad, brothers-mine; She'll help us."

"What makes you so sure?" Rafe asked morbidly.

Carmen sighed. Honestly, she loved these boys, but they could be so *dense* sometimes. "One: She's your Mother, get rid of the self-esteem issues. Second: She's in charge of Heaven, and they're misbehaving. Three: She likes Ro. Can we sleep now?"

Carmen climbed into her bed, not bothering to listen for an answer. She was going to sleep no matter what the others said; they could bother her in the morning.

Ro didn't like mornings.

She was feeling that sentiment very strongly on this particular morning, mostly because she had to get up and deal with what happened yesterday.

She'd been having a lot of those mornings lately.

Ro dragged herself out of bed, her gaze sweeping over Carmen and Gabriel, who of course weren't up yet; she assumed that Luce was making breakfast, as Michael and Raphael's shower things were gone.

She didn't know where God was, and something unpleasant curled in her throat, blocking her air and making it difficult to swallow. Most likely She was with Luce, making breakfast and bonding with Her son—that was never not going to be weird—but all the same…

She should check. Bounding up the stairs, Ro barged into the kitchen without so much as a good morning. God and Luce looked up from the cooker, sheepish grins plastered across their faces. Ro took in the congealed orange lump that used to be beans sitting in the saucepan.

"Really, Luce? What did the beans ever do to you?"

It would be better if she just acted like everything was normal, if she wasn't worried about the Hitgalut Ritual she was supposed to ask God about. In the dream it hadn't sounded so bad, but now that Ro had a few days to think about it, it kind of scared her.

Ro didn't like feeling scared.

"Hey, don't look at me," Luce protested, laughing. "Evelyn said that She would like to cook, and since I figured an almighty being that created the universe shouldn't have too much trouble, I let Her have a go."

"Evelyn?" Ro asked. She thought God would have abandoned Her human name once She got Her memories back.

"There are many gods in creation, just as there are many Gods." The capitalization was audible; Ro was impressed. "Allah, Jah, Ahura Mazda, Waheguru; they are all monotheistic, but all of them have different names. Consider God more of a title." Evelyn glanced at the cooker. "And, ah, sorry about the beans."

"Don't worry about it," Ro said warmly. Evelyn hadn't changed that much, if at all.

"I'm going to go find Mike and Rafe…yeah," Luce said quickly, scampering out of the kitchen before one of them forced him to clean up the mess.

"Coward," Ro called after him teasingly. A bark of laughter floated back up to her.

"You wanted to speak with Me alone," Evelyn said quietly.

Ro sighed and didn't look at Her. "Yeah, I guess. When I was knocked out about a week ago, I had a dream about God. You came to me and told me to ask You about the Hitgalut Ritual. Something about making it worth my while?"

Evelyn said nothing for a long moment, assessing Ro. Whatever She found, it made Her face age about ten years. "You don't know what you are asking, child."

"I'm not a child."

"Everyone says that."

"I'm not everyone."

"No, I don't suppose you are."

"I have suffered more this past year than most people have their entire lives," Ro told Her. "If we measure adulthood by maturity, I have aged beyond my years long ago and a thousand times over." She leaned forward, forcing Evelyn to look her in the eye. "I will do whatever is necessary to keep my friends safe, because they are all I have left. I would rather die myself than see them suffer any longer."

"Suffering is a part of life, you can't change that," Evelyn rebutted.

"Not this kind of suffering," Ro growled. "Not losing everything and constantly running and looking over their shoulders because they're scared of their own family. No one should suffer from that."

"Then they will not," God said simply. "The Hitgalut Ritual, translated into English, literally means Revelation. It transforms higher powered beings to reflect their essence. This spell will restore those true to Me and Mine, and force those who went against us into human forms to live out a mortal life span. It is also known as the Second Chance spell; it gives them a chance for redemption."

"That sounds like a brilliant idea," Carmen yawned, leading the others into the kitchen. "How come none of you told us that?" She turned and poked Gabe in the chest.

"We didn't know such a spell existed," Michael answered, looking at God curiously.

"It is dangerous, and not without faults," Evelyn allowed. "But then again, does any such magic exist, regardless of purpose or power?"

"Great," Ro said briskly. "When do we start?"

"There is only one requirement necessary, and you won't like it," God warned.

Ro snorted. "I don't like anything about this situation. Doesn't change anything. What's the catch?"

"A sacrifice," Evelyn whispered. "A *willing* sacrifice, neither divine nor occult, that still has the power to work the spell. It can be neither I nor My progeny, which leaves you, Rowan, unless you can find another Wiccan of your calibre on such short notice."

"*No!*" came the resounding reply from Carmen and the eldest Elohims.

"Not an option," Luce growled.

"It's not actually up to you lot," Ro snapped, indignant.

"What, so you're just going to throw your life away?" Lucifer yelled, whirling to face her, expression thunderous.

"I'm going to give my life up to make sure everyone else can live like they were meant to!" she replied, furious at his refusal.

"No; nothing is worth that, Ro," Luce said, shaking his head and turning away. "We'll find another way."

"And if there isn't one?" she asked, ignoring the others as they snuck out of the room. Their arguments were starting to become a regular occurrence. "If more people are hurt? What am I supposed to do if one of you is hurt? It will be my fault, and I won't let that happen. *That* is not an option for me, Luce."

"Is there really nothing keeping you here, that you'll just go and end yourself, easy as that?" Luce asked bitterly, still not looking at her.

"How can you not know why I'm doing this?" Ro whispered.

"Why don't you *explain* it to me, Ro?" Luce cried, tugging at his blond hair. "Why could you possibly need to do this?"

"You want to know why it's so easy for me?" she snapped. "It's because there *isn't* another choice. If I don't do this, I'll lose you. Sooner or later, Uriel or someone will get past our defences, and they'll kill you; we can't stay in here forever, Luce. Or the guilt will consume you as the body count ratchets up. I won't let you go through that, not if I can stop it. I have a chance to undo the damage here, and why the hell *shouldn't* I take it?"

"Because I love you!" Luce shouted. "I *love* you, I always have, and I can't lose you either! Did you ever think of that? That you aren't the only one with people you care about?"

"Lucifer," Ro said, tears finally spilling over down her cheeks.

"Don't make me lose you," he said desperately.

Ro pulled Luce around, leaning into him and gripping him as tight as she was able. His arms came up around her, crushing her chest, and yet she was breathing easier than she had in weeks. Luce's tears fell, beading in her hair like salty diamonds.

"Rowan," Luce said hoarsely. "*Please*."

Ro's own tears cascaded down her face as she tugged Luce down. Their foreheads rested against each other as they breathed the same air as naturally as everything else they had ever done. Luce cupped Ro's face, thumbs brushing away the water still leaking from her eyes.

"I can't," Ro whispered brokenly. "I can't, I have to do this, it's for *you*, you stupid prat."

She kissed him, before he could come up with another argument.

She wouldn't lie, thoughts of this more than fleetingly passed through her mind, but it was nothing like she had expected.

It was wet, for one. And neither of them had really had anyone to kiss before, so it was new territory for the both of them.

But it didn't matter how sloppy or awkward it was, or who was the better kisser. This was about reassurance, about love, and all either of them cared about was making the other understand that.

It was the oldest method of communication, and for them it worked just fine.

"Okay," Luce panted. "Okay, I just—"

"Do you want to be with me?" Ro asked. "When it happens? Or is that too much?"

"No. No, I want to be there. I want to hold you, so you know you aren't alone."

"As happy as I am about you two finally getting your act together," Carmen said impatiently from the doorway, the rest of the Elohims and Evelyn hovering behind her, "Ro, are you insane?"

"And you, Lucifer? You're going to let her do this?" Michael asked incredulously.

"Screw you, Elohim," Ro retorted. "No one lets me do *anything*."

"So how exactly do I do this?" Ro asked, nervously twisting her fingers together. Evelyn laid Her hand on top of Ro's, stilling them.

"This entire spell is about instinct, and power. The words are merely to guide you; to successfully activate the Hitgalut, you must be aware of your entire being and devote it to your cause. This is more angel than pagan magic, but—"

"It's like meditation," Ro interrupted softly. "I can do this. What are the words?"

Evelyn smiled sadly at this brave child. "It is not something I can tell you. They are your focus, your centre, and no one knows that better than you. Understand?"

Ro nodded quickly. "Yes. I may need a few days—"

"Take all the time you need," God said. "Spend what time is left with your family."

"Thank you," Ro said, smiling gratefully.

"Do not thank me, Ro." Evelyn shook Her head. "It is I who should be thanking you. You are the saviour of My family and My home; know that you will never be forgotten, and the choirs will sing your name for the rest of time."

"Er…right." Ro stared at Her in shock, making her way out of the room. "I'm just going to…yes. Bye."

Evelyn laughed softly at the Wiccan's awkwardness. Of all people, that girl was perhaps the most extraordinary. Loyal to a fault, extreme power, loving beyond anything She had seen of humans lately. And she admitted to her mistakes, which was hard enough to find among celestial beings, let alone the mortals. Gods and angels and lower deities hated admitting they weren't perfect, and yet this one girl proudly confessed her errors—*and* tried to fix them, which was more than God could say for most of the universe.

Still…it wasn't a bad family Ro made for herself here, far from it. Sometimes, it seemed as if the archangels were closer to the Wiccan than they had ever been to their other siblings. Watching Carmen laugh and tease Gabriel, Evelyn smirked. The girl had no idea of her ancestry, the blood that allowed her to return to Earth. Most people got it wrong.

The Second Coming of Christ was never about ruling Earth, or raising the dead, or judgement. It wasn't about publicity, or creating a new Paradise for everyone. She was here as a leader, yes, but only in case the Apocalypse happened. Once it passed, Her Daughter would lead the world into a new stage of Enlightenment.

Of course, that was all in the future. They had more immediate problems to take care of.

Chapter Seventeen

"Are you sure you want to do this, Ro?" Carmen asked anxiously, brushing her friend's wet curls out. When they were little, they used to practice putting up Willow and Lilly's hair in the traditional braids for casting. Carmen knew it should be Ro's grandmother, or at least her aunt, braiding her hair for the first time. Luce was forbidden to do it, seeing as he wasn't actually a girl, and mentors should by all rights be the only ones to braid. However, lacking a mentor or another female clan member, Carmen was the closest thing to family Ro had at the moment to do this for her.

She was touched.

"Yes," Ro said simply, allowing Carmen to tip her head forward so she could get to the bottom layer of hair. Ro held the rest of the curls up as Carmen wove the few strands into a tight standard braid. Carmen's lips thinned as she tied it off, displeased with the circumstances.

"You shouldn't have to give up everything—" she tried, beginning the French braid.

"I'm not," Ro denied. "I'm not giving up anything; I'm making sure the rest of you don't have to. It's worth it, Carmen, I swear."

Carmen sighed as she reached the nape of Ro's neck, transitioning into the herringbone braid. "I guess. I just don't want to lose anyone else."

"Neither do I," she heard, so quiet she almost missed it. Carmen tied off the end of the herringbone with green silk, winding the small braid around the transition point and tucking the end underneath. She handed the mirror to Ro, watching as she examined her work.

"Amazing," she grinned. "Just like we always practiced."

They had come a long way to be able to speak of their family without falling into depression or bursting into tears. Maybe it was because they knew there was worse to come.

"You shouldn't have to do this," Michael said, pacing back and forth. Raphael leaned against the wall, eyes alternately tracking his older brother and watching Ro calculatingly.

"*Should* isn't really the question here," Ro said calmly, rolling her eyes. "Honestly, it's not like I'm unprepared. I always knew if I manifested there might come a point where I was forced to sacrifice myself for the good of my loved ones or the rest of the world. Are you telling me if it was you, you wouldn't agree without a second thought?"

"Of course I would have second thoughts!" Michael shouted.

"He means," Raphael cut in, "that we don't understand how you could agree so swiftly and completely. Didn't you hesitate at all?"

"Of course I hesitated. I don't want to leave you all. But," she added, holding a hand up to stop Michael's protests, "I can't sit back and do nothing when I have a chance to end this. Now, are you going to mope and be miserable, or are you going to enjoy my last days on Earth with me?"

"This is ridiculous," Michael muttered unhappily, Raphael scowling in agreement. However, they both sighed and nodded. They hardly wanted to let Ro die at odds with them.

"We're all going to miss you, you know. Luce especially." Gabriel peered at her, hoping to spot some weakness he could exploit.

"I know. And I know Luce will be hit the hardest, we've spoken about it," Ro said, moving her black rook three spaces forward. "But loss is a part of life, as the four of you should very well know by now, and while I'm sure it will hurt, you'll get on with your lives."

“Hm. Just because we know it, doesn’t mean we accept it.” Gabriel captured one of her pawns with his bishop.

She promptly stole the piece with her knight. He huffed and frowned at her, trying to guess if she was cheating. “Still, it’s not like we’ll never see each other again. You are archangels, I’m pretty sure that means you can travel to the afterlife.”

“Smart arse,” Gabriel said fondly, taking her rook with one of his. “Check.”

“You love me for it,” Ro said casually, moving her king into place. “Checkmate.”

Gabriel blinked down at the board in confusion, just now noticing the queen poised to kill him—and the assassins cutting off every route of escape. “Did you cheat?”

Ro laughed. “Please. I don’t need to cheat.”

He scowled. “Best two out of three,” Gabriel demanded.

“Prepare to be humiliated, then,” Ro grinned, resetting the board. Gabriel’s eyes narrowed as he smiled sharply.

“Oh, I’m not going easy on you this time.”

“I really don’t like this,” Luce muttered, shifting uncomfortably on the couch. For once, the spell didn’t need fancy sigils or burning herbs—which he was grateful for. It just unnerved him a little. And it smelled funny.

“Stop fidgeting, it will be fine,” Ro scolded, ignoring his disbelieving stare.

“Ro, you are about to sacrifice yourself in an attempt to avert the Apocalypse, and if this doesn’t stop it we are pretty much screwed. You and I have very different definitions of ‘fine.’”

“It will work; don’t you have faith in your Mother?”

“That was a low blow,” Luce muttered sullenly. “What are you doing?”

“Getting a feel for the area,” she replied. “I need to be aware of myself and everything around it for this to work, so the stuff I did before doesn’t count. Everything in this room needs to be accounted for and understood.”

“Everything, huh?” Luce smirked.

She glanced over at him, smiling. "Yes, everything. Wait your turn; I'm saving the best for last."

Luce laughed, and both of them ignored the forced quality to it. "Hurry up, then."

"Yeah, yeah," Ro grumbled, still grinning. She meandered a path that vaguely followed the walls, finally coming to stand in front of him.

"You ready?" she asked, unusually serious and quiet. Or at least, it used to be unusual. Now, it seemed Ro was meek and grave far too often, especially when she should be at her finest, her shining moments.

They hadn't had any *time…*

"No," he replied honestly, and Ro nodded in acceptance.

"Well, the Apocalypse waits for no one," she said, sinking into his arms. Her back was pulled tight to his chest, legs stretched out in front and tangled together. Luce clasped his hands around her waist, afraid if he loosened his hold she would disappear.

He wasn't giving her up that easily.

"Music," she murmured.

Luce frowned. "What?"

"Grandmother always said the strongest magic comes from music, so…"

A low, throbbing hum filled the room, making the edges of Luce's vision pulse with light. Strange, blurred images flickered around the walls. Luce thought they looked a little like people, but their limbs were too long and seemed to have extra joints. The figures were dancing, or perhaps they were fighting. Faint voices rose to join Ro's, and he focused back on the girl in his arms. Though the words were unfamiliar to him, he understood enough to know it was an old Irish folk song of some sort. With each verse, Ro's body tensed, as if the multitude of voices came from her, boosting her power long enough to work the spell. Luce was fairly sure she wasn't calling on the power of her ancestors, because there was no way a human could make noises in that range.

Ro arched in his hold, voice rising as she sang the last verse. Luce caught something about ancient Irish kings, and elves and fairy rings, but for the most part he was concerned about keeping Ro from hurting herself. On the last word—*Donegal*—she folded in half, bent over the circle of his arms.

The last note faded into silence, and Luce barely breathed for fear of breaking the spell. The heavy stillness was layered with emotion; peace, loneliness, hope, fear, joy…and underneath it all, wrath seethed like the riptides of the ocean. Faintly, he could hear Ro humming the first few bars of her song over and over again.

In all the spells Ro had cast before, usually the magic was visible and wild, thrashing around the room. The power here was definitely still present, but it sucked all the air out of the room and crushed them beneath its unrelenting weight.

Luce blinked a couple times, the room getting brighter no matter where he looked.

Probably because the light source was right in front of him.

A halo of white-gold enveloped Ro, pulsing in time with her chanting. *If anyone deserves to be an angel*, Luce thought, *it's the girl in my arms doing everything in her power to save me.*

The light grew, suddenly snapping outwards in a blast reaching far beyond the bunker. Lucifer gasped as it passed through him, feeling like he'd been electrocuted. It rebounded before he collected himself, contracting around Ro in swirling multicolour. Purples, blues, reds, greens, golds, silvers, bronzes, coppers; it was ever-shifting and endless. Faster and faster, the twisting spectrum was about to make Luce sick when it exploded. Again.

He was beginning to see a pattern with magic.

Every nerve in his body shrieked as he was torn from Ro, crashing through the wall and landing in the secondary armoury. Lucifer convulsed, wings tearing from his back and honing to quark-thin edges. He nearly bit through his lip as he flexed muscles long disused. All three pairs had manifested, and the pain was glorious.

He staggered upright, brushing dust out of his hair and shaking an errant blade from his ankle. "Ro?" he called hoarsely, blinking spots out of his eyes. The magic was powerful, no doubt, and he had been human long enough to retain unnecessary habits concerning his body.

His Mother and brothers appeared, Gabriel escorting Carmen. Luce didn't move.

As far as he was concerned, the room was empty of anyone important.

Ro was gone.

Chapter Eighteen

Raven Starwing, heir to the Seelie throne, drifted amongst the stars, fairly sure she wasn't supposed to exist. As the war had drawn to a close, the Seelie Court had prepared to work one of the Forbidden Magicks of their people to save them all. The Unseelie had been vanquished, she knew that much, but why couldn't she remember what had defeated them? Why was her last memory full of blood and pain?

A small tear in the fabric of reality caught her attention. She propelled herself closer, dodging the leaking antimatter. This wasn't right, this was all *wrong wrong wrong*.

Something screamed in the void, sending her fleeing back to the other end of the universe. She flew to the only comfort she had ever known, a small rock of blue and green spinning lazily around the tiny yellow star. Raven aimed for the only Fae-like presence she could find, the brightest one in the cosmos…

Chapter Nineteen

Seven months later…

Carmen burst through the door, Gabriel following close behind. She dumped the bags onto the kitchen counter, slamming her hands down on the table. Luce jerked up and nearly cracked their heads together.

"You are an archangel," Carmen huffed. "Aren't you supposed to have more grace?"

"It's the form," Luce said dully. "Humans aren't as graceful as angels to begin with, and bodies are so confining. It's difficult to transition from pure wavelengths of thought to mortal shells."

"Yeah, well, you lived in that mortal shell for eighteen years before reverting back to your thoughts, Lucifer," Carmen retorted. "And you went through puberty, so you have no excuse. I think Michael and Raphael are glad for those years now; they're training the baby angels, and as hard as they try they will still never be as bad as the two of you."

"Mother kind of turned over all the responsibilities to Mike and Rafe last week," Gabriel continued. "She claimed She was owed a holiday, and not to disturb Her unless the Apocalypse restarted. No one dared contradict Her."

"What is all this?" Luce asked, changing the subject before Carmen and Gabriel began to rant again.

"This is called food, Lucifer," Gabriel said, exaggerating his enunciation. "This is what you have to eat to keep your mortal shell running."

Lucifer frowned at him. "I know that. Why is it here? More importantly, why did it come with an annoying older brother and his girlfriend?"

"We wanted to check on you, make sure you were holding up okay," Carmen called from behind the fridge door. "And by 'okay' we mean not about to off yourself, or do something stupid, or really worse than you were the last time we checked."

"And we received news from hell," Gabriel told him quietly.

Luce's gaze sharpened hopefully. "Well?"

"She's not there. And she's not in Heaven either. Which means..."

"She's still here," Luce breathed, alive in a way he hadn't been since he regained his archangel status. Carmen and Gabriel exchanged doubtful glances.

"Look, Luce," Carmen said gently. "That spell consumed her; it converted all her power to its own. Maybe…maybe we can't find her anywhere because there's nothing to—"

"Stop," Lucifer snarled, eyes wild. "Ro is here, I know it; I can *feel* it!" He whipped around to face his brother. "Gabriel, please—"

"Luce, we're not ruling everything out," Gabe soothed. "But I don't know where else to look. It might just be up to her now."

Luce turned away, defeated and empty once more. "Yeah. Yeah, I guess."

"Oh, by the way," Carmen added. "Gabe is doing the whole book thing. I found his agent, and we're looking for a publisher, and of course it has to be labelled as fiction, but we will it get out there."

"Okay," Luce said quietly, already going back to the books covering the table.

"People will know, Lucifer," Gabriel reassured. "They may not know it really happened, they may not understand it's the truth, but they will know what Ro did. They'll know the story of Heaven and Hell and Earth."

"We stopped the Apocalypse, Luce," Carmen said. "Now everyone will know how."

When he remained unresponsive, Gabriel sighed and steered Carmen towards the door of the bunker. "We'll be by in a few weeks, okay?"

Luce waved a hand at them, blinking blearily at the pages in front of him.

"I'm really worried about him, Gabriel," Carmen sighed, closing the door behind them. The wards Ro put up were still active, if weak, which only further convinced Lucifer she was still here. "He hasn't been getting better, and while we haven't seen him getting worse either, that doesn't mean he isn't."

"I know," Gabriel sighed. "We just have to keep trying, and keep a close eye on him. He lost his mate; angels are lucky if their mind doesn't break from that. The only reason Lucifer isn't insane right now is because he believes there is a chance Ro could come back to him. Until we know for sure, I don't want to be the one to dash that hope and drive him insane."

"You and me both," Carmen murmured. "We have a meeting with the agent in a few minutes; she thinks she has a potential buyer. You want to reschedule?"

"No, I'm good. Ready?"

Carmen grinned. "I love this part. Never gets old."

"You only love me for my wings," Gabriel mourned. Carmen's laughter echoed in the forest, even after the pair had soared away.

Raven stood across from Lucifer, arms crossed and scowl firmly in place.

"You are an idiot, Lucifer Morningstar," she informed him. He didn't react.

"What are you doing, moping around here? Get your act together," Raven tried again. Still nothing. Raven threw her hands up into the air and heaved herself onto the table. Crossing her legs in front of the archangel, the young Fae snapped her fingers and waved her hands in front of his face.

When that garnered no reaction, she huffed. "Typical. I don't know why I expect anything different after seven months of this nonsense. Oh, wait: you're an archangel. You're *supposed* to be intelligent and sensitive. I guess everyone got it wrong."

She stared at him. He stared at the wall. She rolled her eyes.

"Well, now what am I supposed to do? And you, being completely unhelpful." Raven frowned at Lucifer, who had now gotten up and wandered out of the room. She hopped down and followed him, trailing his footsteps down to the library. She sighed in exasperation as Lucifer made his way back through the stacks. The table at the very centre was the one the archangel had spent the most time at, and it was the one the archangel went down to now.

Judging by the clothes and blankets and garbage strewn around, the angel spent a lot more time than she thought down here. She sighed and crossed her arms again.

"Look at this mess. Is this how you treat a library? Honestly, leaving rubbish everywhere like this. And sleeping down here, really? That sounds more like something I would do when I was just a Faeling..." Raven trailed off as Lucifer grabbed books seemingly at random from the nearest shelves. On closer examination, they were from all over the library, and seemed to be collected and stacked within easy reach.

"What did you do, screw up the entire organization system?" she wondered, leaning against the nearest bookshelf. Raven watched as Lucifer half-heartedly picked up the papers and wrappers on the floor. "At least you're starting to clean up after yourself. I was beginning to worry you wouldn't be able to do anything on your own."

The archangel thumped down into his chair, dragging the closest tome in front of him. He caressed the cover once before opening it to a well-marked page. Raven peered at it and groaned.

"Really, Lucifer? Spectre Summoning? You are an *archangel*. Can't you just go to the afterlife if you want to talk to somebody that badly?"

"Where are you, Ro?" Lucifer muttered, propping his head on his palm. The side of his face smeared up, hair mussed and matted down from its usual spiked state.

"What did your family call you? Luce?" Raven wondered. "Is that her name for you? This girl you are so obsessed with?" She waited. No reaction. She sighed again. "I am sure this maiden of yours is worthwhile, but I have not crossed universes simply to be ignored by one of the only beings that may be able to help me. Your family is the most powerful on Earth, and my family *needs your—*"

With a sickening lurch, the darkness surged around her and yanked her back *again*, tossing her across galaxies to witness the beginning of the end. She tumbled through time and space, inexorably drawn back to the void. It had grown wider every time she returned, always with more of the viscous absence of everything spewing from its gaping maw.

The screams were growing closer, flashes of lightning and fire sweeping past the opening at irregular intervals. One managed to slither out, zipping past her and vanishing in between two solar systems. It looked vaguely humanoid, in the same way a spark of fire looked like a raindrop. Exact opposites, and only one had any semblance of form. Dread pooled in the Fae princess' belly, and she turned to face the beginning of a nightmare.

A deep roar underscored the piercing shrieks. Deep wingbeats reverberated through the universe, nearly shaking Raven to pieces. A giant form loomed behind the rip, somehow managing to distinguish itself from the backdrop of dark matter. Clawed wings grasped the edges of the tear, splitting it further and heaving its massive bulk through. Atop a head as big as Earth's sun, a regal figure stood swathed in shadows. Golden hair whipped at her face, tawny eyes narrowed in distaste at the complicated mess the Deities had made of everything. They had infected the cosmos with their ideals and practices and followers, destroying everything she and the Unseelie had worked for.

More dragons and their riders dragged themselves through to this reality, thousands more foot soldiers spilling out around them. Raven gasped and shrunk back in fright, the sound and movement catching the hawk eyes of the first. The young Starwing was frozen in place for a few seconds before having the presence of mind to escape, but it was long enough. The Queen of the Unseelie had seen her, and recognized the age-long threat to her and her people.

Raven appeared in front of Lucifer once more, struggling to stay in one place, let alone speak to the archangel. Even so, there was no guarantee that he would ever be able to hear her, anyway.

She still had to try.

"Lucifer Morningstar, *please*, I need you to listen to me," Raven begged, hating herself for the action even while she knew that there was no other choice. "The Unseelie are back, I don't know how because they should all be dead and gone and they are coming here and *why won't you listen*?"

She fell back with a sob, landing in the chair across from him but still not able to interact with Lucifer the way she wanted to—the way she needed to. "What are you even looking at, you fool?"

He turned the page, skimming along something that was apparently supposed to help connect with a loved one telepathically. "You don't want that; empathic bonds are better, it's harder to lie. Anyone can pretend to be someone telepathically, if they're powerful enough and they are given enough motivation. Better add a truth spell in there, just to be sure. Unless you angelic lot already come premade with built-in lie detectors."

Lucifer frowned and closed the book, opening the spiral-bound one beside it and jotting down a few notes. Raven leaned forward curiously, gaping in shock. Lucifer had written down almost exactly what she said, which meant he could hear her, which meant—

"Lucifer," she said excitedly. "Luce, I need you to—"

He stood up and walked away, obviously doing something more important than listening to a supposedly dead Seelie princess telling him about another possible *Armageddon*.

Angels had no respect for anyone these days. On that note, perhaps one of his older brothers would listen to Raven. Or the Christian God. She just hoped Christian deities didn't get territorial, like some other religions she could name.

Heaven looked…surprisingly normal, if freakishly clean and unblemished. From humanity's descriptions, she had expected it to be all pompous and self-righteous in its extravagance.

Apparently humans had no idea what they were talking about. Not that that was new.

She flew on whatever was keeping her afloat, surprised that she could manipulate another domain, all the way to the giant flat-topped pyramid in the centre. She figured it was a safe bet; usually, the massive structure smack bang in the middle of the city was important in the grand scheme of things.

Raven made a mental note never to use the phrase 'smack bang' again. Even in her head. And to stop adopting human quirks.

She slipped through the top, more evidence of her apparent welcome here grinding her teeth together. The place was fuller than she expected; their God paced around the base of a smaller centre pyramid crowned with a platform in a tight, restless circle, changing directions every few revolutions. St. Michael and St. Raphael leaned against their columns, and St. Gabriel stood halfway between his pillar and the strange centrepiece.

He had his human mate with him too, and Raven was surprised that she wasn't more surprised.

"I don't suppose it's too much to hope any of you can hear me?" Raven asked, already resigned to the fact.

No response. Of course not. That would be far too easy.

"I'm worried about him," the human (*Carmen*) said, watching the God pace. "He hasn't been sleeping well, or eating, and he's not taking care of himself."

"I think he noticed our concern the previous visit, and so I'm pretty sure Lucifer took a shower just before we got there," St. Gabriel reported. "Otherwise, I don't think he could care less about his own health."

"He's obsessed with getting Ro back," St. Michael put in quietly. "I am worried he might go…alternative routes if it meant he had a second chance with her."

"He bloody well better not," Raven growled. "I will kill myself if he does. He has a slightly more important job than trying to bring back some mortal girl. Besides, the universe is destroying itself quite happily without his help."

"He should be up here, with the rest of his family," St. Raphael sighed. "We can help him, in a way that does not risk him or the balance of the rest of the universe."

"That's a good plan," Raven agreed. "Let's go with St. Raphael's plan. Then maybe one of you will *listen to me*."

"I don't think he will succeed," the God said softly. "Ro is beyond any of our reaches, even mine, and if she did somehow survive, the rest is up to her."

"Thanks for that, Yahweh," Raven frowned at Her. "What is so special about this girl that all of you are so focused on finding her?"

Yahweh paused and seemed to stare right at her. Raven held her breath hopefully, wishing and believing for just a few seconds…

Until She shook Her head and moved on. Raven stuck her tongue out at the back of Her head in a fit of protest. If a supreme monotheistic God couldn't tell she was there, then who else was supposed to help her?

Raven shivered at the memory of the malevolent Queen. She had looked right at her, had apparently seen *and* heard her, which didn't bode well for Raven and the rest of the universe. She was going to have to keep searching until she found someone else, someone who she would be able to interact with and work with her and not stab her in the back—or in general—the first chance they got.

Perhaps she could try the pagans. Raven had Kali's amulet, for some reason, and the Fae did have some alliances with pagans. They didn't care about them as long as none of the Court problems affected pagan followers, but would occasionally help the Seelie Court keep the Unseelie in line.

Raven clasped the talisman in her hand, focusing on the power signature embedded within it. A trace of magic threaded across the world, grounding itself in India. Raven followed it quickly—and ended up on top of Mount Everest.

Naturally.

Kali stood on the ledge above her, arms outstretched and hair flaming in the wind. The snow blurred the vision enough that the afterimage of two more sets of arms joined the first. Raven shivered, bothered by the extreme cold even with her level of tolerance and her current state.

She hated being incorporeal. She kept walking through things. That always brought on the unsettling sensation of being split apart into little tiny bits. Walking through some*one* was even more disturbing, since it felt like she was being absorbed and separated and rearranged all at the same time.

She didn't really like it, but it was surprisingly easy to get used to. Enough that the amusing reactions of people when she did it made up for the unpleasantness. They always jumped about a foot in the air.

"Kali?" she shouted, voice snatched away by the wind. She tried again, climbing closer. When that didn't work either, Raven tried to reach out to her—only to pass right through her, and Kali *didn't even notice.*

Raven screamed in frustration and threw the amulet at the goddess, launching herself into the air as far as possible without getting herself slingshot back towards the void by whatever force kept bringing her there. She figured if she stayed close enough to Earth, she wouldn't be noticed as much.

Of course, she was just shooting in the dark again. She had no bloody clue what caused her to come and go, but it was really pissing her off. If this was someone's idea of a joke, she was launching one of the Fae's infamous prank wars, and they would see exactly how funny something like this could be when they got age-old mischief-making beings involved.

Not paying attention to where she was going, Raven barely blinked when she hit the first trees. Even with woods around, she could spot human civilization on the edges, as well as a sign proclaiming the area to be Central Park. Alright then. Raven shrugged and went with it. Things couldn't get worse, could they?

Chapter Twenty

Raven wandered into a random drinking establishment, frustrated after another failed attempt to communicate with someone. No matter what she did, nobody could hear or see her, even if sometimes she thought she was getting through. She had tried everything she could think of, and not even the more sensitive mediums among humans could perceive her.

She blinked at the dim interior, wondering why, if she was incorporeal, her eyes still had to adjust to the lighting. Raven squinted at the patrons, wondering if she could play any pranks here…

At the end of the counter, two figures with unpleasant angel-turned-mortal auras sat, apparently drowning themselves in liquor. Raven wondered how much they knew about the limits of the human body, especially where drinking was concerned. She walked over to the fallen angels (*Uriel* and *Kokabiel*, the distressed auras whispered to her), not bothering to dodge patrons or waiters or furniture anymore when she could pass right through them. Raven stopped behind them, deciding not to announce her presence.

"Bloody witches," Kokabiel snarled. Except he was so deep into his cups that it came out sounding more like 'Vlggdy guiches.'

"You're telling me," Uriel slurred. His enunciation was a little better, but not by much. "When I find that bitch I'm going to flay the skin from her bones."

"If you mean who I think you mean, you might find that a little more difficult than you thought," Raven told him, absently peering at the alcohol board. She had never wanted to drink human alcohol, weak as it was, while she was Fae, but there was nothing quite like dying without ever trying something and then going around seeing it everywhere to make you miss it.

And that was the first time she'd admitted, even to herself, that she had probably died during the end of the war and that was the reason for her current state of body and mind.

She was distracted by Uriel letting out a very unmanly scream and Kokabiel falling off his stool in a drunken heap.

"Is this what they were talking about, the hallucinations?" Kokabiel mumbled, her appearance seeming to have sobered him up some.

"What hallucinations?" she asked curiously. Seriously, what had the former angels been doing, going out and abusing every narcotic and alcoholic substance known to mankind while the Unseelie were breaking reality?

"You're a hallucination," Uriel told her gravely.

"You can see me?" Raven was stunned. This was a new development.

And probably the universe laughing its arse off at her. Of course the only people she could communicate with were former angels with a drinking problem that appeared to be on a hunt for revenge, most likely for that girl everyone was so concerned with.

"And hear you, unfortunately," Uriel muttered, while Kokabiel grinned dopily up at her.

Definitely narcotic abuse.

"Okay," she said slowly. "That's new."

"Wayzat?" Kokabiel asked, pulling himself up by the counter edge. Uriel didn't help him up.

"Well, I think I'm supposed to be billions of atoms scattered through time and space, but somehow I ended up as this instead," Raven explained, bemusedly watching Kokabiel's perilous adventure up the stool.

"A ghost?" Uriel suggested snidely.

"Do I look like a ghost to you?" Raven asked, offended. She thought angels knew what spirits were, and how they acted, and she was nothing like them, thank you very much! "Fae do not become ghosts when they die! That's a human thing." Raven wondered why the fallen angels looked so stricken. Hadn't they ever met a Fae before? "Besides, did you miss the 'scattered through the cosmos' part of the explanation? I wasn't just talking about my physical body; my mind and soul were a part of that too. Or rather, that's what happens when a Fae dies normally. I guess me and normality are just not meant to be."

"Nothing's meant to be," Kokabiel said, waving a finger in her face. "The whole bloody Apocalypse was ripped off because you decided it wouldn't be any fun. Well, *you're* not any fun!" He nodded decisively and leaned back—promptly toppling off the stool again.

"You should get sobered up," Raven told him, ignoring the clearly insane angel and turning back to Uriel. "Why did you want to start the Apocalypse, anyway?"

"To get rid of all the humans," Uriel moaned. "Then Lucifer would come home and everything would go back to the way it was supposed to be."

Raven slapped him upside the head. Uriel gaped at her. Kokabiel appeared to be passed out at their feet.

"You moron," she hissed. "I've been out of it for a few centuries and I didn't actually care about your religion in the first place—actually, I still don't—but even I know that Lucifer only left his home because most of Heaven was too stupid to understand the depth of his love. He is more than capable of loving all angels and all humans equally; you lot just didn't give him the chance to. You are lucky the bloody Apocalypse was stopped; Lucifer would never have rested until you and your followers were dead. And his brothers would have helped him."

"Oh," Uriel said miserably. Raven huffed.

"Yes, quite. Now, help me get this fool to wherever you two are staying, and then we need to talk. We have bigger problems than your family issues to deal with now."

Uriel reached down and grabbed Kokabiel's arm, touching Raven's shoulder with his free hand. The young Fae bowed her head in concentration, and in a whirl of stardust, they vanished from the bar.

The few patrons that caught sight of the pair (Raven was still unfortunately out of sync with most of the universe) thought they had lost count of their pints, and simply shook it off as another odd occurrence. It was New York, after all.

Coming Soon!

Don't miss the sequel of *Revelation*! *Genesis* brings us in a full-circle, back to the very beginning.

Rowan Fitzgerald is dead, the forces of Heaven and Hell are scattered, and the Unseelie Court has been unleashed. The spell that restored the archangels undid the Bindings on the Fae, and the Unseelie Queen is hunting for the Seelie Court. Meanwhile, Seelie Princess Raven Starwing remembers nothing since the last days of the war, and the new world she's found herself in needlessly complicates her life. All she knows is that her Court is gone, the Unseelie are free, and new deities have emerged. If she is to win this battle of the Fae, she must accept their help, no matter how suspicious she finds them.

Lucifer has withdrawn, choosing to walk the earth instead of returning to Heaven. He searches for some sign that Ro isn't gone for good. His brothers and Carmen have been looking for every angel that Fell, beginning the slow process of redemption. Demons are being herded back into Hell by the other angels, and it is being repurposed as a place for second chances instead of eternal punishment.

Carmen has been torn between looking after her best friend's family and focusing on the bigger picture. Clean-up is a huge job, but she can't believe Ro is dead and gone. The last spell Ro worked *did* something to her, awakened some long-dormant gene, *changed* her somehow. Carmen needs to find her friend and get answers.

The Unseelie Queen wants revenge for her imprisonment. The only Seelie Fae left is the Heir to the Court: Raven Starwing. The only obstacles are the strange new beings that are fighting so fiercely to protect her. Still—for all the centuries her Court spent tearing itself apart, she will return the damage hundred-fold to the princess and all she holds dear.

About the Author

Rhiannon Davies grew up in Saint Louis, Missouri. In her spare time, she rides and trains horses, and volunteers out at Longmeadow Rescue Ranch. She has always loved to read and write, and has worked on many different projects, though *Revelation* is the first she has published. Rhiannon likes to look at traditional stories from a different perspective, which is part of the reason she decided to write the two-book *Faith* series.